DANGER – MARMALADE AT WORK

Marmalade Atkins is the naughtiest girl in all the world. She puts herself about appallingly. Her parents have given up. Teachers refuse to teach her.

But grown-ups will be grown-ups and the social workers are still out to get Marmalade. This time it's keen, trendy Wendy Wooley putting all her training and the best caring the caring profession can offer into a new idea: the *Work Experience Scheme*.

Marmalade is let loose on the outside world. She joins the army, she joins the police force. She goes to art school, she goes to cookery classes. She even becomes a trainee social worker!

But do you think she becomes a good girl . . . ?

Cover shows Charlotte Coleman as Marmalade Atkins in the Thames TV series Danger – Marmalade at Work.
Executive Producer: Pamela Lonsdale
Producer: Marjorie Sigley
Directors: John Stroud and Peter Duguid

D0488793

Danger –
Marmalade at Work

ANDREW DAVIES

(Illustrated by John Laing)

A Thames Magnet Book

Also in Thames Magnet
MARMALADE ATKINS IN SPACE
MARMALADE ATKINS' DREADFUL DEEDS
EDUCATING MARMALADE

Magnet paperback edition
first published 1984
by Methuen Children's Books Ltd,
11 New Fetter Lane, London EC4P 4EE
in association with Thames Television International Ltd
149 Tottenham Court Road, London W1P 9LL
Reprinted 1984 (twice)

Published simultaneously in hardback by Abelard Schuman Ltd
Text copyright © 1984 Andrew Davies
Illustrations copyright © 1984 John Laing

Reproduced, printed and bound in Great Britain by
Hazell Watson & Viney Limited,
Member of the BPCC Group,
Aylesbury, Bucks

ISBN 0 423 00840 4

Contents

Bad Girl Warning

TO PARENTS:
Most of us dream about doing bad things and putting ourselves about. This book is about a girl who really does do bad things and really does put herself about. She does not come to a bad end. She does not reform. She just goes on being bad. In fact, she gets worse. You would be advised to keep this book away from your children.

TO BAD GIRLS (AND BOYS):
This is the book you want.

Marmalade Atkins, Social Worker

Marmalade Atkins was in a cage. It was a small cage with stout iron bars, and she couldn't get out of it. She had growled and she had yowled and she had paced up and down, and once or twice she had managed to grab her father through the bars and bite big holes in his Harris Tweed jacket, but she couldn't get out. She was trapped, and Mr and Mrs Atkins were feeling very pleased with themselves.

How it came about was like this: Mrs Atkins had had the bright idea of sending to Harrods for a small leopard to keep Marmalade in order during the long summer holidays. But after three days the leopard was looking very sorry for himself, and pining for a nice quiet zoo. He had never met anyone like Marmalade Atkins before. So one day, when Marmalade was showing the leopard how to tie reef knots in his tail, Mrs Atkins opened the cage door, let the leopard out, and shut Marmalade in. The leopard went lolloping off to terrorise the countryside, and Marmalade was a prisoner.

Mr Atkins bought himself a lion tamer's hat, and tried to train Marmalade by bribing her with pork pies and poking her with the stick he kept to poke pigs with. It was not a great success.

"Grrrrr!" growled Marmalade, seizing the end of the stick in her teeth and dragging Mr Atkins up against the bars. "No one is going to tame this girl, cock!"

"Tell you what, Muriel," said Mr Atkins, as he mopped

his brow and fell into an armchair. "We could paint a few spots on Marmalade and send *her* back to Harrods. They might fall for it."

"Atkins, you are a hopeless dreamer," sighed Mrs Atkins, opening a new box of chocolates from Fortnum and Mason.

"Anyway, cock," said Marmalade. "I'm not spending the rest of my life doing leopard impressions. You ask Mrs Allgood."

At that very moment, the doorbell rang, and the Atkinses heard a lot of shrieking and growling coming through the letterbox.

"Help! Help! Let me in!" wailed a despairing voice.

"Funny," said Mr Atkins. "Sounds like her now." And he went to the front door and let Mrs Allgood in.

Mrs Allgood was Marmalade's social worker and she was not looking at her best that morning. Her flowery hat was in tatters, there was a large jagged hole in the back of her dress, and her understanding smile was rather lopsided. She had in fact just fought a furious draw with the leopard in the front garden, but she was much too polite and ladylike to mention this. And she also had a secret, which was such a wonderful secret that even fights with leopards didn't seem to matter any more. The secret was that this was her very last day as Marmalade's Social Worker!

"Well," said Mrs Allgood. "How are we all getting on?"

"Terrible, cock," said Marmalade. "Look what they've done to me! Putting girls in cages, I ask you, is that right?"

"No, I don't think it is, dear," said Mrs Allgood. "But it's no skin off my nose!" And she smiled a smile that was not a bit like her usual sympathetic understanding one. It was more of a mad carefree grin. Mrs Allgood was not very good at keeping secrets, and she was so excited that she began to skip and dance about the living room in her sensible social worker's shoes.

"I've been promoted, I've been promoted!" she sang, "and you're not my little client any more!"

"Mrs Allgood," said Mrs Atkins in a trembling voice, "am I to understand that you are leaving us in the lurch?"

"That's right, that's right!" sang Mrs Allgood.

"But what's going to happen to our poor little girl?" said Mr Atkins, trying to sound forlorn and pathetic.

"She's going to have a new social worker!"

"What sort?" said Marmalade suspiciously.

"One of the new sort, dear! You'll see!" And Mrs Allgood skipped off to begin her new job. On the way down the path she gave the leopard such a hefty whack with her social worker's handbag that he decided not to terrorise the neighbourhood any more and went to give himself up at the nearest police station.

Mrs Allgood went straight back to the office, handed in her social worker's kit, her social worker's hat, and her giant bulging file on Marmalade Atkins. Then she put on a white coat and a smart peaked cap, picked up a tall striped stick and marched off to start her new life as a Lollipop Lady. She enjoyed stopping the traffic so much that in her very first week she caused a traffic jam that stretched from Birmingham to Exeter, when a hedgehog went to sleep on her Zebra crossing.

Next morning, Marmalade's new social worker arrived at the Atkinses' house. She wasn't a bit like Mrs Allgood. She was young and keen and trendy and very very eager to help people. Her name was Wendy Wooley and she thought everything was super. She wore dungarees and a woolly jumper and a woolly cap and her round innocent eyes peered out through a fringe of woolly fair hair.

"Gosh! Super! Wow! Terrific!" said Wendy Wooley. "Super to meet you, Marmalade!"

9

Marmalade stared at her new social worker. She looks just like a sheep in a romper suit, thought Marmalade to herself. Now Marmalade Atkins is not like you or me. When she thinks this sort of thing she usually says it out loud.

"You look just like a sheep in a romper suit," said Marmalade to Wendy Wooley.

"Marmalade!" hissed Mrs Atkins.

"Gosh!" said Wendy Wooley. "Isn't she good at sharing her feelings? Oh, Marmalade, we are going to have fun!"

Mrs Atkins sighed. Why did social workers have to be so soft?

"What sort of fun, cock?" said Marmalade. "Sheepdog trials?"

"No!" said Wendy Wooley. "I've got the most marvellous scheme for you!"

"What sort of scheme?" said Mr Atkins suspiciously. "Can't be another school. She's been thrown out of more schools than I've had hot dinners." (This was perfectly true, and you can read all about these schools in a book called *Educating Marmalade*.)

"No," said Wendy Wooley. "It's a wonderful new scheme, and it's supported by the Government! You see, kids who don't get on well with schools, kids who are, shall we say, a little *difficult* . . ." (Mrs Atkins gave a hollow laugh) . . . "can learn to be good and useful citizens in the World of Work! Yes, Mr and Mrs Atkins, I'm talking about . . . Work Experience!"

"What sort of work?" said Marmalade suspiciously.

"Something absolutely ace!" breathed Wendy Wooley, beaming at Marmalade through her shaggy fringe. "Social Work!"

"You mean like you, cock?" said Marmalade in disbelief.

"Gosh, she's so quick, isn't she?"

"You mean I can go and muck about in other people's

10

houses?" said Marmalade.

"Right! Super! Except we don't call it Mucking About, we call it Relating to the Client! Finding out his needs! Helping him cope!"

"Eating his chocolate biccies!"

"Gosh, right, wow, yes!" said Wendy, blushing slightly because she had just absentmindedly finished a whole plateful of Fortnum and Mason's Choice Chocobix. "Only we call it 'Sharing with the Client on a one-to-one basis'!"

"I call it taking diabolical liberties," said Mrs Atkins sourly.

"Well, gosh, anyway," went on Wendy hastily, "I'm sure you'll have a super fantastic time, and I've got you an absolutely super fascinating client of your very own! What d'you say?"

"All right, cock," said Marmalade. "I'll give it a whirl."

"Super!" cried Wendy Wooley. "Open the cage!"

The next morning, there was Marmalade Atkins, Trainee Social Worker, trudging down a grotty old back street to find her client. Wendy Wooley had kitted her out in Mrs Allgood's old outfit: social worker's hat — flowery; social worker's shoes — sensible; and a social worker's kitbag — full of safety pins, headache pills, worry beads, and tissues to cry into. The street was long and grimy and full of small shabby houses, and right at the end of the street was the smallest and shabbiest house of the lot. Mr Machonochie's house.

Wendy had told Marmalade about Mr Machonochie. "You'll like him, Marmalade. He's an absolutely ace old gentleman," she had said, with a smile that seemed more sly than understanding. But that would be impossible, because social workers are never sly.

Marmalade banged on Mr Machonochie's door. No answer. She banged again.

"Go away!" growled a hoarse voice from inside.

Marmalade opened her Social Worker's Handbook to see what to do next. It told her on Page Two.

"Cooee! Mr Machonochie!" trilled Marmalade in her best imitation of Mrs Allgood. "I'm your new social worker and I've come to help you with your problems!"

"I havenae got any problems," roared the voice. "You come in here, Jimmie, ye'll have problems! I'll nut you like I did the other one!"

Marmalade threw her Social Worker's Handbook in the gutter, where a passing tomcat dodged it, sniffed it, rejected it, and went on his way.

"Oh, come on, cock!" she yelled through the letterbox. "I only want to muck about!"

The door opened instantly and Marmalade found herself looking at a very small, whiskery old Scotsman with a huge flat cap on his head.

"Mucking about, is it?" said Mr Machonochie. "Why did ye no say so before? In with ye!"

Mr Machonochie liked mucking about just as much as Marmalade did. First they had a short boxing match, and when Mr Machonochie had finished wheezing and coughing, they decorated his living room. They did this by squirting paint through Marmalade's water pistol, and when they had finished, the walls, ceiling, furniture, Marmalade, Mr Machonochie, and Mr Machonochie's cat were all covered in bright splodges of red, yellow and blue.

"Ah, Jimmie," sighed Mr Machonochie, sinking into his newly decorated armchair. "I havenae enjoyed meself so much since Granny caught her nose in the mangle. You're a real good social worker, Jimmie Marmalade. What shall we do now?"

"Well," said Marmalade. "In this book I threw away, it said find out what the client needs and help the client

12

achieve it."

"That's easy," said Mr Machonochie. "I wantae rob a bank. I havenae robbed a bank since 1943. That was when I was Mean Machonochie, hardest man in Glasgow."

"I don't think social workers are supposed to do that," said Marmalade, who privately thought it an excellent idea.

"You listen to me, Jimmie," said Mr Machonochie. "We're robbing the rich to help the poor, like Robin Hood!"

"Who's the poor?" said Marmalade.

"Us," said Mr Machonochie. "Besides, that's what I wantae do, and you're supposed to help me. I wantae rob a bank, and I havenae got a gang!"

"All right, cock," said Marmalade. "You've got one now."

Just before closing time that afternoon, Mr Machonochie and his social worker walked into the High Street bank, grim and determined. They were in full bank robbers' kit: striped jerseys, black masks, with swag bags over their shoulders and water pistols in their fists. They marched straight up to the lady cashier (a nice plump lady called Miss Peach) and stood on tiptoe to see over the high counter.

"Hello, dear!" said Miss Peach. "What a sweet little outfit! How can I help you?"

"This is a stick-up, Jimmie!" roared Mr Machonochie.

"Yeah, hand over the money, cock!" yelled Marmalade.

"Mr Plum! Mr Plum!" called Miss Peach. "We're being stuck up! I mean held up! The manager won't be a moment, dear," she added to Marmalade. "Sorry to keep you waiting."

A large pink man in a large blue suit came out of the manager's office rubbing his large white hands. "Oh, I say, how jolly!" beamed Mr Plum. "What sweet little chaps! Are you the cubs? Bob a job week again already?"

"We're not cubs, we're bank robbers, ye silly Sassenach!"

growled Mr Machonochie.

"Yeah! Open the safe!" growled Marmalade.

"Oh, golly, Miss Peach, what a charming charity stunt," beamed Mr Plum. "Of course we'll contribute. Where are your collecting boxes, my little man?"

"You don't understand, cock," raged Marmalade. "This is the real thing!"

"Yes of course it is, here's ten pence for you and ten pence for your little friend here. Now run along, there's good boys!" And he picked them up by their collars and carried them out on to the pavement.

"I'll get you for this, Jimmie!" snarled Mean Machonochie.

"Yeah, we'll be back, cock," shouted Marmalade as the big glass doors closed in her face.

"I think the younger generation are just wonderful," said Miss Peach.

"Ten pence is an insult, Jimmie," said Mr Machonochie when they had got home. "I've let ye down. I'm just a poor old feller who cannae do the business any more." And tears filled his eyes.

"Cheer up, Mr Machonochie, cock," said Marmalade, handing him the box of Social Worker's Tissues (Extra Strength) to cry into. "We'll find a way. Hey, I saw this film once on telly."

"Hey, I saw one of them!" said Mr Machonochie. "They tunnelled in!"

"Aye, they did! Through the sewers!"

Mr Machonochie fetched a large shovel and a small shovel from his shed, and he and Marmalade started to dig a hole in the middle of the living room floor. It was a long tough job, but Marmalade and Mr Machonochie were a couple of dedicated criminals, and with only a couple of breaks for

Extra Strong Tea from Mr Machonochie's tea caddy and Comforting Biscuits from Marmalade's Social Work Kit, they had tunnelled through to the main sewer by ten o'clock that night. Ten o'clock at night? But weren't Mr and Mrs Atkins pacing the floor and worrying about what might have happened to their little girl, out and about so long after bedtime? No they weren't, I'm sorry to say. They had forgotten all about her. But what about Wendy Wooley? Wasn't she worried sick about the outcome of her Work Experience Scheme, and the fate of her little client? No, she wasn't. She had other things on her mind. That very night, she and Dr Glenfiddick, her boss, were playing snooker for the Social Services against the Police Force. It was a very important match, and the honour of the Helping Profession was at stake. Wendy Wooley was so proud and excited that she invited Mr and Mrs Atkins to the Police Station to watch her play. And *still* no one wondered what had become of Marmalade.

Marmalade and Mr Machonochie were plodding along through the knee-deep murky water in the main sewer. The tunnel was dark and eerie, and large whiskery rats scampered along the black greasy walls and swam busily about in the scummy stream. Marmalade and Mr Machonochie didn't mind the rats or the scummy stream. They both had their wellies on, and Marmalade had her Bad Girl's Torch.

"Got tae watch out for alligators down here, Jimmie," said Mr Machonochie, his voice echoing spookily. "Awful fierce, them alligators."

"Alligators? You must be joking, cock!"

"No, Jimmie, that's the only snag with these sewer jobs, losing your way and getting ate by the alligators. Aside from that it's a doddle."

Marmalade shone her torch all round, but there was no

sign of alligators. Instead, high up on the wall, was a little round door like the cover of a manhole. And on the door were the words: HIGH STREET BANK.

"We made it, cock!" said Marmalade. "Shall I stand on your shoulders or will you stand on mine?"

In half a minute they were in the dark, deserted bank, and Mr Machonochie danced up and down with glee, leaving black smelly footprints all over the carpet. Then he stopped and hit himself on the head.

"Marmalade, I've let ye down," he said. "I've forgot the jelly."

"Never mind, cock," said Marmalade. "We can buy all the jelly we want when we've got this safe open."

"*Gelignite*, Jimmie. Is this your first bank or what? The jelly's to get the safe open!"

"Stand aside, Machonochie, cock," said Marmalade. "I've got the Special Social Worker's Safety Pin!"

Marmalade took the Special Safety Pin from her Social Worker's handbag, and twiddled it in the lock. And to Mr Machonochie's amazement, the great steel door swung slowly open!

"Oh, Jimmie Marmalade, you brought joy to an old man's heart!" said Mr Machonochie as they shovelled the bundles of notes into their swag bags. "Now, back down the sewer and we're home and dry!"

But somehow the sewer looked different on the way back. The rats were scampering and swimming about as merrily as ever, but there seemed to be too many turnings, too many dead ends with muck and rubbish sloshing drearily against blank, dank walls. After a while the intrepid bank robbers realised that they had lost their way.

"Cheer up, cock!" said Marmalade. "At least we haven't met any alligators!"

Just as she spoke, a dreadful croaking sound like the

opening of a huge rusty box echoed down the tunnel.

Marmalade shone her Bad Girl's Torch ahead of her. Nothing happened for a moment or two, then a huge head about three feet long with wicked eyes and two great rows of gleaming teeth appeared around the corner.

"Oh, blimey, it *is* an alligator!" said Marmalade.

"Oh, blimey, it's Marmalade Atkins!" said the alligator, and scuttled off down the tunnel.

"Follow that alligator!" cried Marmalade. "He'll know the way out! Come on, Mr Machonochie, cock!"

Meanwhile, in the hushed atmosphere of the Police Station Social Club, Wendy Wooley was about to pot the final ball that would give her victory over Sergeant Sprodd, and bring fame and honour to the Social Services.

"Keep calm, Miss Wooley," whispered Dr Glenfiddick, who was trembling like a leaf himself. "There's a box of chocolate eclairs for you if you can only pot this black!"

Wendy Wooley leaned over the table and took careful aim. Her eyes were steady and bright, her hand was firm, and her feet were standing on a little round metal plate, rather like the cover of a manhole. Just as she drew her arm back to play the final shot, the cover of the manhole shot upwards. Wendy Wooley was catapulted on to the table, and the black ball flew into Mr Atkins's open mouth.

"Seven away! The Police win!" said Sergeant Sprodd.

"Where am I? Where am I?" said Mr Machonochie, emerging from the hole and gazing about wildly.

"I know that cap!" yelled Sprodd. "That's Mean Machonochie! Seize him, lads!" Six burly policemen chased Mr Machonochie round and round the table. Snooker balls and policemen's helmets were flying everywhere.

"What's going on, cock?" said Marmalade, coming out of the hole dripping with slime.

"Marmalade!" shrieked Mrs Atkins.

"We're in the nick, Jimmie!" gasped Mr Machonochie. "Back down the hole with ye!" And he dived down himself head first.

"Follow him, constable!" yelled the sergeant.

"Over my dead body!" said Marmalade. "He's my client!"

Then a horrible croaking sound came from the hole and the alligator stuck his head out. Mr Machonochie's cap dangled from one side of his jaws and a few mangled notes dangled from the other. The alligator burped loudly.

"Oh, dear," said Marmalade. "What *have* you done?"

"He's eaten the money!" moaned Sergeant Sprodd.

"Think he's eaten Mr Machonochie too," said Marmalade. "And I think I'd better be off now."

19

Private Marmalade

It was a peaceful scene in the Atkins house. Mr and Mrs Atkins were drinking tea and gobbling rum truffles in the living room, while Marmalade was playing with her new toys. It all seemed too good to be true. And it was.

"Marmalade," said Mrs Atkins. "Those rum truffles are for ladies to nibble at, not for little girls to throw about."

"What rum truffles, cock?" asked Marmalade.

Mrs Atkins took a closer look at the rum truffle in Marmalade's grimy hand, and then at the toy gun on Marmalade's shoulder, which suddenly didn't look like a toy gun any more. Then she dived for the telephone.

"Hello, Harrods!" she shrieked. "You've made the most terrible mistake! I ordered lemonade and trifle, not grenades and a rifle!"

Marmalade pulled the pin out of the grenade, tossed it over the back of the sofa, and stuck her fingers in her ears. "Bet it doesn't work, anyway," she said. But it did.

The following afternoon, Wendy Wooley came to tea with the Atkinses. The rum truffle grenade had caused surprisingly little damage. There was quite a draught from the hole in the wall, of course, and the sofa had disappeared, but Mr and Mrs Atkins looked years younger without any eyebrows, and it was great fun sitting on packing cases and tea chests instead of chairs.

"One thing you learn in Social Work," said Wendy Wooley, "is that things aren't always what they seem. And every problem's an opportunity in disguise."

"Come again, Wend?" said Mr Atkins.

"Well, gosh, what I think is . . . she's just trying to show affection in her own special way! She wasn't trying to blow you up, honestly! She was making a plea for love and attention!"

"See your point, Wend," said Mr Atkins doubtfully. "Very deep, that. But couldn't she just have sent us a Valentine Card, sort of thing?"

"Look, gosh, I know you're feeling just a little bit miffed, but all this has given me an ace new idea for Marmalade's Work Experience! Something where she can really put herself about!"

"Now you're talking, cock," said Marmalade. "Have a rum truffle?"

"Gosh, super, thanks," said Wendy Wooley. "I really shouldn't . . ." The rum truffles looked rather large and metallic, and Wendy couldn't see very well through her shaggy fringe.

"No, you really shouldn't!" yelled Mr and Mrs Atkins, diving for cover.

"Super great big ones," said Wendy Wooley, taking one.

"You just pull that little stalk thing out," said Marmalade helpfully.

"No! No!" screamed Mr and Mrs Atkins.

Wendy Wooley pulled the little stalk thing out.

When the smoke had cleared, Wendy Wooley was still sitting on the edge of the tea chest. Most of her clothes had gone, and her face was black with soot, but she still had that eager trusting smile on her face.

·"What I had in mind, Mr and Mrs Atkins," she said,

"was the Army." Then she closed her eyes and toppled slowly off the tea chest on to what was left of the carpet.

First thing next morning, Mr Atkins took his little girl down to the Army Recruiting Office, and there, below a poster telling you how you could put yourself about in the modern army, sat Sergeant Major Spratt. He had a face like a giant tomato, bright blue glaring eyes, and a moustache so huge and stiff you could hang out the washing on it (which is what he sometimes did on active service).

"And what have we here?" he bellowed delightedly. "I will tell you what we have here! We have two lovely recruits what wants to serve their Queen and Country!"

"One lovely recruit," said Mr Atkins hastily. "I've done my bit, squire! Now it's the turn of the younger generation."

"And what's your name, my lovely?" said Spratt, turning a horrible smile on Marmalade.

"Marmalade Atkins, cock. What's yours?" The sergeant major's eyes bulged a little wider. "I am Sergeant Major Spratt, and that is what you will call me, my lovely boy, because when little squaddies call me cock, d'you know what I do with them?"

"Pat 'em on the head and give 'em a biscuit, cock?"

"No, my lovely, I bites their little heads off and spits out the pips!"

"Do it! Do it!" shouted Mr Atkins excitedly.

"I'm off to join the Navy," said Marmalade, making for the door.

"No, no, no, just my little joke!" boomed Spratt, hauling her back by the collar. "Haven't signed the forms yet, have you? No, all good pals in today's army, my lovely boy. It's all ping pong and sing song and jolly japes in tents!"

"You sound like a great big softy, cock," said Marmalade.

"Oh, I am, my lovely boy," said Spratt craftily.

22

"Now look here, squire," said Mr Atkins, who didn't much like the sound of all this. "What I want to know is, is the training tough? I mean, do you make 'em march till their toes come through their boots, do you make 'em polish buttons till they're crosseyed, do you tear their arms and legs off if they're cheeky?"

"Oh, no, nothing like that," said Spratt, winking craftily at Mr Atkins. "It's all teddy bears and bedtime stories now. Mind you, he is a bit short. You sure he's over sixteen?"

"You must be joking, cock," said Marmalade. "And I'm not a boy either!"

Mr Atkins put a bundle of pound notes on the desk.

"Right, sign here," said Sergeant Major Spratt. "Twenty years."

"Twenty years?" said Marmalade. "What if I don't like it?

"Too late now, my lovely boy," said Spratt. "You're in the Army now!" And before Marmalade knew where she was, she found herself in a huge cold drill hall with a lot of other new soldiers who all looked much bigger and tougher than she was. Sergeant Major Spratt issued Marmalade with one uniform, baggy; one pair of boots, clodhopping; one rifle, heavy; one pack, very heavy; and one hat, silly.

"Now, my lovely boys!" roared Spratt. "I will tell you what you are going to do. You are going to march till your toes come through your boots, you are going to polish buttons till you are crosseyed, and if you are cheeky I am going to tear your arms and legs off. Any questions?"

"Yes, cock," said Marmalade. "Has anyone ever told you you look like a beetroot with a moustache?"

Sergeant Major Spratt's face went so red with rage that he looked like a beetroot with a moustache.

"Ooh, my lovely boy, we're going to have some fun with you," he roared. "Squad! At the double on the spot ten miles running go!"

Marmalade found herself pounding up and down between two enormous soldiers, while Sergeant Major Spratt went off for a nice cup of tea.

"Here, cock," said Marmalade. "This is terrible. Don't you ever get tired?"

"Not us, shorty," said the soldier on her left.

"'Cos we are tough!"

"Yer, and hard," said the soldier on her right. "He's Private Tuff and I'm Private Hardman!"

"Yer," said Private Tuff. "And we're not only tough and hard, we are thick as well. Sergeant Spratt said so," he added proudly. Marmalade had an idea.

"Here," she said. "I bet you're not thick enough, I mean I bet you're not tough enough to carry your packs and rifles and me as well."

"Yer, we could, we could do that easy!" boasted Private Tuff and Private Hardman.

"Don't believe you," said Marmalade. When Sergeant Major Spratt came back from his nice cup of tea to see how his brave lads were getting on, he found Private Tuff gasping for breath ("I'm clobbered, Sergeant!") and Private Hardman buckling at the knees ("I'm kippered, Sergeant!") but strange to tell, Private Marmalade didn't seem tired at all.

"Right my jolly boys!" said Sergeant Major Spratt. "Polishing the shiny buttons go! One two, one two, one two, one two . . ."

Marmalade lay on her bunk reading the Beano while Private Tuff and Private Hardman polished buttons so hard that they went crosseyed. After a while they were so crosseyed that they didn't realise they were polishing Marmalade's buttons instead of their own. When Spratt came round to inspect them he was most impressed.

"Private Tuff and Private Hardman," he said. "Look at the shine on Private Marmalade's buttons! You can stay up all night, my jolly boys, and polish till your buttons is as bright as what hers is!"

In the morning, it was Unarmed Combat, but poor Private Hardman and Private Tuff were so clobbered, kippered and crosseyed that they could scarcely stand up, let alone fight.

"Right, my lovely lads!" roared Sergeant Major Spratt. "Unarmed Combat, into the centre rush, last man on his feet is the winner, putting yourselves about, GO!"

Private Tuff and Private Hardman stumbled, clobbered and kippered to the centre of the gym, banged their heads together and collapsed in a heap. Private Marmalade sat on top of the heap and fanned her face with the Beano.

"Unarmed Combat, cock? Easy!" she said.

"Private Marmalade," said Sergeant Spratt. "You have vandalised two of my best men. There is only one thing to do with you!"

"Whassat then, cock?"

"I am promoting you to patrol leader in the SAS!"

"What do they do, cock?"

"The SAS, my jolly boy, are the hardest and the fittest and the toughest men in the whole army. They storm embassies, they run in and out of people's houses shouting FREEZE, they swim thousands of miles with knives between their teeth — all because the lady wants a box of chocolates . . . it's a great honour I'm offering you!"

"Good old Private Marmalade!" gasped Tuff and Hardman.

"*Corporal* Marmalade, now," said Sergeant Spratt.

Mr and Mrs Atkins were delighted when they heard how well Marmalade was getting on in the army. Mrs Atkins ordered three new fur coats from Harrods, and put them all on at once to celebrate, and Mr Atkins bought himself a new Rolls Royce and drove it down to the Suparich Gulf State

Embassy in Mayfair, where he was hoping to sell Nelson's Column to the Sheikhs for three hundred camels.

His business deal went very well, and he was just working out the final delivery details with the Chief Sheikh (it is not an easy matter to transport three hundred camels on the tube to Trafalgar Square) when two enormous men brandishing giant leeks leapt in through the window.

"Afternoon, gents," said Mr Atkins. "These your camel wallahs then, Sheikh el Shifteh?"

"No! No!" quavered the Sheikh, cowering under the ottoman. "I have never seen them before! They are bandits!"

"Throw down your weapons, boy bach!" said the first enormous bandit.

"Unless you want a leek across your chops, look you!" said the second enormous bandit.

"Look, squire," said Mr Atkins, falling on his knees. "No need to be hasty. I'm sure we can work out a deal on this one!"

"No deals," said the bandits. "We are seizing this Embassy in the name of the Welsh Liberation Front!" And waving their leeks above their heads, they sang two rousing choruses of *We'll Keep a Welcome in the Hillsides*.

"Er, look, squire," said Mr Atkins politely, when they had finished. "I don't want to cause any aggravation, but I think you might have made a blunder. This is not the Welsh Embassy you've seized here. How about trying next door?"

"We know it's not the Welsh Embassy! We know all that, boyo! That is the whole point of what we are doing, look you! We haven't got an embassy of our own to seize, so we're seizing this one. Well, it was the first one we come to, see. So it's the Welsh Embassy now! All right?"

"All is now clear," said Mr Atkins, who was no fool when it came to business. "How would you like to buy Nelson's Column? I'm letting it go cheap today. How about four hundred sheep?"

Meanwhile, back at SAS headquarters, the jolly boys were waiting for their first mission. They were all ready, kitted out in balaclavas, wet suits, goggles and flippers. They had parachutes, ropes, guns, knives and chocolate boxes. But it was a quiet day for emergencies. No one had invaded the Isle of Wight, no one had seized London Airport, and there didn't even seem to be any ladies in castles wanting chocolates.

"Keep on your toes, my lovely boys," said Sergeant Major Spratt. "The SAS are always on their toes!"

"Blinking difficult in these flippers, cock," said Corporal Marmalade.

"But if that red alert goes, my jolly boys, we shall shoot into action like corks out of ginger beer bottles!" And even as Spratt spoke, the red telephone rang!

"Suparich Gulf State Embassy, lads!" said Sergeant Spratt. "And don't forget the chocolates!"

Mr Atkins was just working out the final details of his deal with the Welshmen.

"Right, squire, four hundred sheep to travel first class on the Cardiff express, arriving Paddington three o'clock tomorrow afternoon," he was saying, when there was a huge crash, followed by the sound of splintering glass, and the Gallant SAS squad swung through the Embassy window on ropes.

Unfortunately, in the excitement, Private Tuff and Private Hardman had put their balaclavas on back to front. It is also very difficult to storm an Embassy in frogmen's flippers.

"Freeze!" they yelled, and stumbled blindly across the room and straight out of the opposite window. Sergeant Major Spratt found himself standing between two giant Welshmen, evil smiles on their faces, giant leeks poised to strike.

"Steady on, boys," said Spratt apprehensively.

27

"No violence. I'm a bit on the Welsh side myself."

Two giant leeks swung simultaneously, and Spratt sank lifeless to the carpet.

"Now for the dwarf in the flippers!" said the Welshmen, turning their attention to Marmalade.

"Let's have you then, Taffy," said Marmalade.

Now Welsh bandits are a bit impulsive and excitable, and these two really should have stopped and thought that Marmalade was two feet shorter than Sergeant Spratt. But they didn't. Two giant leeks swung simultaneously into two Welsh heads. And two Welsh bandits fell in a heap on Sergeant Major Spratt's unconscious body.

"Mission accomplished!" said Marmalade, taking off her balaclava.

"Marmalade!" said Mr Atkins.

"Hello, Dad. Fancy a chocolate?"

"Well, I'll . . . I don't know what to say," gasped Mr Atkins.

"Say nothing, Dad. And now I must leave you. I have other worlds to conquer. The Army is too soft for me. Goodbye!"

And clinging to the rope with her flippers, she jumped out of the window and was gone.

"Well, I never," said Mr Atkins to the astonished Sheikh who was crawling out from under the ottoman. "My little girl!" he said proudly. "Fancy a choc, Sheikh?"

They both took one.

"Funny," said Mr Atkins. "These remind me a bit of those rum truffles we . . ."

I expect you remember the pictures of the explosion at the Embassy on the TV news, and how they said it was something to do with a Top Secret mission, and the story could never be told. Well, now you know what really happened.

What the Butler Saw

Wendy Wooley was thrilled with Marmalade's Army exploits, but her boss, Dr Glenfiddick, the head of the Social Services, was not. "Something must be done about this girl, Miss Wooley," he said, twiddling his toes irritably in their yellow socks.

"But something *is* being done!" she cried defiantly. "My work experience scheme is making us famous!"

"Your work experience scheme is making us a laughing stock, Miss Wooley. So far, your little client has robbed a bank and blown up a very nice embassy!"

"Well, I'm on her side," said Wendy Wooley. "Trouble with you is you don't understand the younger generation, cock!" She stopped and put her hand to her mouth. "Oh, dear! What have I said?"

"Miss Wooley," said Glenfiddick ominously. "You are letting your little client influence you. I've seen it all before. Any more of this and it'll be Meals on Wheels for you."

"Big bully," muttered Wendy Wooley.

"I beg your pardon?"

"Oh, I was just wondering what you had in mind for Marmalade next?"

"Something," said Dr Glenfiddick, "where she can learn the old-fashioned virtues of Hard Work and Obedience! We are going to put your little client into service!" And he waved an advertisement which he had cut from the pages of

The Lady. "Listen to this: Wanted, young girl of good family for the post of third kitchenmaid, snivelling skivvy and general dogsbody at Artichoke Hall! Ha ha! That'll teach the little monkey!"

Artichoke Hall was a Stately Home. It was so stately that the front drive was four miles long, and Marmalade was glad that she had her roller skates on as she carried her little case up to the enormous front door. The vast bulk of Artichoke Hall loomed above her.

"Cor," said Marmalade. "Plenty of scope for putting meself about in there!" And she rang the bell.

The door was opened by Mr Portnose the butler. He was very tall and very stout and very smart in his butler's uniform, and he looked at Marmalade down his enormous red nose.

"You rang, madam?" he said.

"Right on the button, cock," said Marmalade. "I'm Marmalade Atkins, come to put meself about!"

Portnose crooked his finger and Marmalade came closer. "Get round the back, you snivelling little brat," he said. "I shall inspect you in your uniform in one minute flat, in the servants' kitchen!" And he slammed the door in her face.

One minute later, all the servants were lined up in their uniforms for Mr Portnose's inspection.

"Welcome to a life of slavery in the servants' kitchen!" said Portnose. "Curtsey to Mrs Bridgeroll, Head Cook and Housekeeper!"

"Skinny little thing, ain't she, Mr Portnose?" said the plump housekeeper.

"Keep her that way, Mrs Bridgeroll. Cabbage water soup is the diet for skivvies!"

"Here, lay off, cock," said Marmalade. "Bangers and mash is what I have!"

"Three pence off your wages for cheek, Atkins," said Portnose. "These are Scrape and Toady, first and second footmen respectively." Two huge men in tight breeches grinned nastily down at Marmalade.

"Look like a couple of giant frogs to me, cock," said Marmalade.

"Another three pence off your wages for cheek," said Portnose. "Aggie and Maggie, first and second kitchenmaids! Stop that snivelling and wipe your noses, Aggie and Maggie. 'Till now your lives have been a misery, now you have the chance to take it out on this little worm — Marmalade Atkins, third kitchenmaid, dogsbody, and general slave!"

"Ooh, Aggie!" said Maggie, cheering up.

"Ooh, Maggie!" said Aggie, wiping her nose on the corner of her apron.

"Aggie and Maggie, three pence off your wages for speaking out of turn!" said Portnose, and they both started snivelling again. "Now Atkins, your duties consist of scrubbing floors, cleaning boots, washing dishes, and having your skinny little bottom kicked by anyone who's in the mood. Keep your head down, your nose clean, and never go in the Butler's Pantry. Any questions?"

"Yes, cock," said Marmalade. "Is that your nose or has someone stuck a strawberry on your bonce?"

"Dogsbody Atkins!" thundered the butler. "Six pence off your wages for gross insolence! And that's three months wages gone so far. I leave her in your care, Mrs Bridgeroll. I am going into the Butler's Pantry and I don't wish to be disturbed."

By ten o'clock that morning Marmalade had scrubbed three floors, cleaned twenty pairs of boots, washed sixty dishes, and had her skinny little bottom kicked ten times.

"Ah, my dear," said kind Mrs Bridgeroll, giving Marmalade's skinny little bottom an extra kick for luck in passing, "it seems bad now, and it'll be worse yet, but t'aint the end of the world. I was once third kitchenmaid myself, would you believe that? Yes, my dear, I dare say in time, if you scrub hard, they'll consider you for *second* kitchenmaid! Now what do you think of that?"

"Not a lot, cock," said Marmalade. "There's only one job I fancy in this place, and that's the butler's!"

"Butler, indeed!" said Mrs Bridgeroll.

"Butler indeed!" said Scrape and Toady the footmen, laughing so much they had to hold each other up.

"Well, how do I get to meet Lord Artichoke then?" asked Marmalade. They were all just starting to laugh and hold each other up again when a bell on the wall started to jangle.

"Lawks a mercy, that'll be him now, wanting his breakfast!" said Mrs Bridgeroll. Aggie and Maggie loaded the great silver tray with devilled kidneys, kedgeree, seven kinds of sausages, scrambled eggs, a few steaks and chops, and three kinds of sauce. While they were doing this, Marmalade crept under the table and put her roller skates on.

Just as Scrape and Toady were poised to take the tray, Marmalade pushed off from the sideboard, skimmed gracefully between them and sailed through the door with the tray, shedding showers of sausages as she went.

"Stop her! Stop her!" yelled Mrs Bridgeroll. Scrape and Toady rushed to the door, collided, and knocked themselves out.

"Lawks a mercy!" cried Mrs Bridgeroll. "Whatever will Mr Portnose say?"

Upstairs, Marmalade pushed open the great double doors of the breakfast room, and glided in. There sat Lord and Lady

Artichoke, one at each end of a table about twenty yards long.

"Breakfast is served, my lord!"

"Ay say Mabel!" said Lord Artichoke. "The butler's shrunk! Must have been left out in the rain, haw, haw, haw! Never mind, serve up the kippers!"

"I'm not the butler, I'm the new kitchenmaid. Marmalade, cock!"

"On the kippers? What a novel idea, haw, haw, haw!" said Lady Artichoke. "Come on then, serve it up! We're famished!"

Marmalade soon found that serving breakfast to Lord and Lady Artichoke was not an easy matter. They were both very greedy, and both very impatient, and they were sitting such a long way apart. Marmalade found herself hurtling up and down the table at forty miles an hour with kippers, kedgeree, sausages, bacon, devilled kidneys, scrambled eggs flying in all directions. In the end, when both the Artichokes called for tomato sauce at the same moment, Marmalade sat down in the middle of the table and directed one squirt at the Lord and one at the Lady. Both her shots were good shots, but she got the people instead of the plates. It was then that Mr Portnose came in, his great red nose quivering with rage.

"Portnose," said his lordship, licking tomato sauce off his moustache, "what is the meaning of this?"

"Dreadfully sorry, my Lord," said Portnose, catching Marmalade by the scruff of the neck. "A little *fracas* below stairs. I shall take this little monkey away and lock her up. It won't happen again."

"Want a bet, cock?" said Marmalade, as Portnose carried her out under his arm.

"Rum little beggar," said Lord Artichoke when the door had closed.

"Quaint little midget," agreed Lady Artichoke. "What's the programme for today?"

"Guests for dinner, my dear. Lord and Lady Parsnip are coming round, I'm hoping to sell them a Rembrandt painting for half a million smackeroos!"

"But we haven't got a Rembrandt painting," said her ladyship.

"Yes we have," said Lord Artichoke. I painted it myself yesterday. Parsnip won't know the difference. Besides, we need the money. All the antiques and silver keep disappearing."

"Very rum, that," said Lady Artichoke. "Ah well, anyone for croquet?"

Meanwhile, in the Atkinses' living room, Mr Atkins was very busy. He was just putting the finishing touches to a painting of a big bowl of flowers. It wasn't a very good painting, but Mr Atkins was very pleased with it. With his tongue sticking out of the corner of his mouth, he carefully painted a signature in the corner: VAN GOFF.

"Atkins," said his wife. "Just a teeny question. Have you gone completely bonkers?"

"Not a bit of it, my dear," said Mr Atkins. "I am going to sell this Van Gogh to Lord Artichoke tonight for half a million smackeroos! He won't know the difference, and besides, we need the money. Now don't forget. I'm Lord Parsnip, and you're Lady Parsnip!"

"Oh, Atkins!" shrieked his wife. "Sometimes you have the sweetest ideas!" And she picked up the telephone and ordered a new diamond tiara from Harrods.

Marmalade was locked in the butler's pantry. She was not only locked up, she was chained to the wall. Now this would upset Aggie or Maggie, or even you or me, but it didn't bother Marmalade Atkins at all. She had been locked up by experts before. (For example, in Bad Girl's Cupboards, dormitories, even Dartmoor. You can read about that in *Educating Marmalade*.) The chain might be thick and heavy, but it was also long. She spent a couple of hours exploring Portnose's pantry, and found some very interesting things. Legs of chicken, bottles of pop, and jellies and trifles. When she had dealt with these, she found some more interesting things: a large collection of antiques and silver, and a box full of disguises. Portnose was not just a butler and a bully. It seemed he was a crook as well! Marmalade had another leg of chicken and some more pop and sat down to have a think.

When Portnose at last went to the pantry to see if Marmalade had learnt her lesson, the other servants heard a lot of bangs and crashes and howls and groans coming from behind the green baize door.

"Ooh, Aggie!" said Maggie.

"Ooh, Maggie!" said Aggie.

"He must be giving that little monkey a right seeing to!" said Mrs Bridgeroll with satisfaction.

Everything went quiet then, and after a few minutes the green baize door opened, and there stood a very small figure with a large moustache and wearing a butler's uniform several sizes too big.

"Good ah evening," said the small person, bowing. "Mr Plotnose unfortunately indisposed. I am new ah Japanese butler. I serve ah dinnah now yes please velly quick chop chop!"

And the new Japanese butler walked calmly past Mrs Bridgeroll and the footmen, and went upstairs to the dining room.

Mr and Mrs Atkins were having a whale of a time. Mr Atkins was in full evening dress (with the fake Van Gogh under his arm) and Mrs Atkins was wearing *two* tiaras (she hadn't been able to decide which one she liked best).

"Bottoms up, Lord Artichoke!" said Mr Atkins, swigging down a glass of champagne.

"What a quaint expression!" said Lady Artichoke. "Bottoms up to you, Lord Parsnip, haw, haw, haw!"

"See you're interested in art, Artichoke," said Mr Atkins, looking at the fake Rembrandt on the wall.

"Yes, yes, that's a jolly old Rembrandt, might have to let it go cheap, half a million smackeroos, y'know!"

"Ay say squire, what a jolly old coincidence!" said Mr Atkins. "Ay just happen to have this very fine Van Gogh I was thinking of disposin' of for the very same sum!"

"My lords, ah ladies," said Marmalade. "Dinnah is ah served!" And she bowed low.

"Who the devil are you?" said Lord Artichoke.

"Plotnose ah have to lie down cock. I am ah new Japanese butlah at your service sah." Mrs Atkins thought there was something strangely familiar about the new Japanese butler, but she was far too polite to say so.

"Well, shall we all sit down?" said Lord Artichoke.

"Bottoms down, Lord Parsnip haw, haw, haw!" said Lady Artichoke. And they all sat down at the great long table.

"OK folks," said Marmalade. "Now you see ah superfast Japanese service!"

The superfast Japanese service went very well, considering. Marmalade skated rapidly round the table serving bird's nest soup, noodles, and Japanese raw fish with abandon. A surprising amount of it went on to the plates, but unfortunately Mr Atkins was sitting at an awkward corner where Marmalade had to take the bend on one skate, and by the time the meal was served, the front of his dinner jacket was festooned with loops of damp noodles, and a fishy eye stared out from his buttonhole.

"First class work, Shorty," said Lord Artichoke.

"Now, Artichoke old boy," said Mr Atkins.

"Yes, Parsnip old stick. I say, didn't realise you were wearing your decorations haw, haw, haw!"

"About the fakes, I mean the paintings," said Mr Atkins.

"Well old chap, I've had rather a beezer wheeze," said Lord Artichoke craftily. "Why don't we swap? I've been a bit brassed off with the old Rembrandt lately . . ."

"And while I'm heartbroken to part with the Van Gogh, squire . . ." (Little does he know I'm getting a masterpiece and he's getting a jolly old fake, thought Mr Atkins).

"Jolly good, Parsnip!" (Little does he know he's getting a jolly old fake and I'm getting a Van Gogh, thought Lord Artichoke).

Just as they were shaking hands on the deal, the great double doors flew open, and in staggered Portnose in his underwear with a big lump on the top of his bald head.

"Portnose!" shrieked Lady Artichoke. "What is the meaning of this?"

"I'll kill that little monkey if it's the last thing I do!" snarled the crazed butler.

"Ah so blimey!" gasped the Japanese butler and dived under the table. Portnose dived after her.

"I say! Cabaret! Haw, haw, haw!" said Lady Artichoke.

"Got you!" growled Portnose under the table. But it was dark down there, and one ankle is much like another in the dark.

"Someone's going to pay for this!" yelled Mrs Atkins, as she disappeared beneath the tablecloth.

"Got you!" growled Portnose again, and Lord Artichoke went under like a diving whale.

"I must see what's going on under that table haw, haw,

haw!" laughed Lady Artichoke!

"Sounds like fun," agreed Mr Atkins, and down they went. Marmalade was the first to emerge, with Portnose close at her heels, brandishing a giant salami.

"Ah so!" hissed Marmalade. "Japanese karate chop!"

The giant salami split in two, and Portnose staggered backwards, grabbing at the tablecloth for support. Just as the Artichokes and the Atkinses were crawling out on their hands and knees, the end of the table collapsed, and the tablecloth, candelabras, plates, glasses, raw fish, noodles and soup slid slowly down on top of them.

Marmalade bowed. "Will you be requiring anything further, sah? No? Ah so. Japanese butlah bids you all honourable goodbye!"

And Marmalade Atkins, Japanese butler extraordinary, skated gracefully away into the night.

Marmalade Bravo

"Anybody there?" called Wendy Wooley through the letterbox. "Super! I've brought someone to see you! Can we come in?"

"Be a Dobermann Pinscher I expect," said Mr Atkins hopefully. "He'll keep you in order girl!"

"Ah so," said Marmalade thoughtfully, and Mrs Atkins gave her a piercing look. She still had her suspicions about the Japanese butler.

As soon as Wendy Wooley came in, Mr Atkins dived straight over the back of the sofa.

"This is Chief Superintendent Thumper," said Wendy proudly. A groan came from behind the sofa.

Chief Superintendent Thumper was a large man in a large uniform. He had shiny silver buttons and a shiny pink face. "Afternoon all," he said.

"May I introduce Mrs Atkins?"

"Charmed, I'm sure," said Marmalade's mother.

"And this is little Marmalade!"

"Wasn't me, cock," said Marmalade hastily. "I was no-where near the place, honest guv, it was two other butlers!"

"Belt up, Marmalade," said Mrs Atkins briskly.

"Thank you, Madam," said Chief Superintendent Thumper. "And where is Mr Atkins?"

"Well, Superintendent, he's, er, he's . . ."

"He's gone to Saudi Arabia!" said a voice behind the sofa.

41

"He's gone to Saudi Arabia," said Mrs Atkins.

"Then may I ask what you are concealing behind that sofa?" asked the superintendent shrewdly.

"Er . . ."

"A duck!" said Marmalade.

"Quack, quack!" said Mr Atkins.

"I see, Madam," said Thumper. "Well all that seems perfectly in order."

"You must be even dafter than you look, cock," said Marmalade.

"In any case, Madam," Thumper went on, "my visit does not concern Mr Atkins but the little girl here."

"Oh, hello there squire!" said Mr Atkins, popping up immediately. "I just got back from Saudi Arabia y'know, terrible place squire, all sand and no booze, fancy a drink?"

"Not on duty," said Thumper.

"Well, excuse the pong of camel dung," said Mr Atkins, gabbling on in a panic. "Plane was full of 'em, couldn't see the movie for the humps. Well, don't want to keep you, I expect you want to take our little girl away and use minimum force on her. Well, say no more, do your worst, I think our policemen are wonderful!"

Chief Superintendent Thumper looked at Mr Atkins thoughtfully. "Sort of a loony, your husband, is he Mrs Atkins?" he asked.

"How wonderfully perceptive of you, Superintendent," gushed Mrs Atkins. "Take him away!"

"Mr and Mrs Atkins, please!" said Wendy Wooley hastily. Superintendent Thumper isn't here on a criminal investigation!"

The whole Atkins family sighed with relief.

"No, no, no!" Wendy continued. "It's a super new development of my Work Experience scheme! Superintendent Thumper will explain."

"Well, it's like this," said Thumper ponderously, bending his knees and flexing his truncheon. He was not very good at explaining things; what he liked was locking people up. "It's like this. The police force, believe it or not, has been coming in for a bit of stick lately."

"Disgraceful!" said Mrs Atkins.

"Yes," said Thumper. "It's been handed down from the top that we are out of touch with the public. Not enough minorities on the force, whatever they are. We have got to recruit some different types."

"What sort of types, cock?" said Marmalade.

"Well," said Thumper. "It seems there's not enough *very short* people in the police force. Not enough *girls*. Not enough *cheeky little monkeys*."

"I begin to see your drift," said Mrs Atkins.

"Marmalade Atkins," said Chief Superintendent Thumper. "How would you like to be a copper?"

"Would I get a big blue hat, cock?" said Marmalade.

"You would."

"And a truncheon?"

"And a truncheon."

"Superintendent Thumper, cock — you're on!"

Next morning, Marmalade arrived bright and early at the police station for her police training. She had an extra tall helmet to bring her up to regulation height, and a lovely shiny new truncheon swinging from her belt. She felt very excited as she lined up with Constable Whacker and Constable Prod.

"Now, Constables Whacker and Prod," said Thumper, "this here may look to you like a nasty little girl dressed up as a bobby, and that's exactly what it is!"

"And this here may look to you," said Marmalade, "like a pig in a peaked cap, but it's not, it's dear old Superintendent

Thumper!"

"Ooh, sir!" said Whacker and Prod.

"It's the new police image," said Thumper gloomily.

"Now let us see if you have mastered the Police Handbook. All constables, Police Talking begin!" And Whacker, Prod and Marmalade lined up and recited together:

"Hello, hello, what have we here?
A likely tale, oh dear, oh dear!
Turn out your pockets please, sign right here,
Is this your car, well blow in here,
And if you want to know the time ask a policeman!"

"Very good," said Thumper. "Walkie talkies!"
All the constables whipped out their pocket radios, and recited:

"Tiger to Octopus, got a bit of bovver here,
Requesting assistance, going down the chipshop,
How's your Auntie Mabel, shame about her kidneys,
Tiger to Octopus, over and out!"

Chief Superintendent Thumper nodded in a pleased sort of way.
"Well done lads, that's quite satisfactory, not bad at all, now you got me doing it, pull yourself together man . . . All constables: Police Walking begin!"
Police Walking consisted of slow plonking up and down in a straight line, with special attention to knee bending, looking left and right, and truncheon twirling. Marmalade managed very well, except that her truncheon seemed to have a life of its own.
"Please sir!" said Prod. "Atkins keeps poking me!"
"Creep!" said Marmalade.
"Silence in the ranks!" said Thumper. "Constable Marmalade! You have passed your test in Police Walking and Police Talking. I now pronounce you fit for duty."
"Oh, brill," said Marmalade. "Does that mean I can go and put meself about now?"
"Certainly not, Constable. Your duties are a making of the tea and a watering of the plants."
"You must be joking, cock," said Marmalade. "I don't *do*

45

that sort of thing. I muck about!"

"If it's good enough for Juliet Bravo, it's good enough for you!" thundered Chief Superintendent Thumper.

"Nice cup of tea, this, Super," said Constable Whacker ten minutes later.

"Yer, Super, lovely strong flavour," said Constable Prod.

Chief Superintendent Thumper smacked his lips. "Delicious!" he said. "This is the best tea I've ever had in this nick — Sergeant Marmalade!"

"Blimey!" said Whacker and Prod. "'E's promoted 'er!"

It wasn't until they'd got to the bottom of their cups that they found the dead mice.

Marmalade's next task was watering the station plants, and the station plants were in a sad state. They were feeble, wispy little things, dropping pathetically over the edges of their pots. Marmalade gave them a good talking to.

"Call yourselves plants?" she said. "What's the matter with you? Put yourselves about a bit! How about a nice cup of station tea and a few Bad Girl Bullseyes?" And the plants pulled themselves together in no time.

"Here, Super, look at them plants!" said Constable Whacker.

"Right big hairy plants, them!" said Constable Prod.

"Those plants there," said Superintendent Thumper, "are the best plants I've ever seen in any nick in England — Inspector Marmalade!"

"Blimey!" said Whacker and Prod. "'E's promoted 'er again!"

Now that she was an Inspector, Marmalade set some changes in motion. She gave courses in Police Joking (Where do all the policemen live? Ledsby Avenue!), Police Rollerskating on the Beat, and Police Bubblegum Blowing.

"This is the life, eh, lads?" said Marmalade.

"This is the life, Inspector," said Thumper. "But . . . well, I don't like to criticize, but there is one snag."

"What's that then, cock?" asked Inspector Marmalade.

"Well, it's just a small detail, like," said Thumper apologetically, "but w're not making any arrests. We're not catching any criminals! The cells are empty!"

"Not surprised at all," said Marmalade. "This nick's not cosy enough. I mean, who'd want to spend their time in cold, damp draughty old cells?"

"Got a point there, Inspector," said Thumper.

"And the food in this nick is rotten too!" said Marmalade.

"Yer, that's right," said Whacker. "Greasy stew!"

"Yer, that's right," said Prod. "Lumpy potatoes!"

"Permission to get things sorted out sir?" asked Marmalade.

"Permission granted," said Chief Superintendent Thumper.

So Marmalade got on the blower to Harrods, and in no time the cells were full of large comfy sofas, four poster beds, imitation log fires and well-stocked cocktail cabinets. Large vans rolled up at the back door loaded with champagne, smoked salmon, lemonade and icecream. And very soon large queues of criminals formed at the desk, all of them confessing to many crimes, some of which they had not even committed. By the next evening, the cells were full of jolly burglars eating, drinking and blowing bubble gum. Inspector Marmalade's plan had worked.

Wendy Wooley rushed round to the Atkinses with the good news. "Gosh, super, wow, you're not going to believe this!" she panted. "Marmalade's been promoted to Inspector already, and Superintendent Thumper's absolutely delighted with her!"

"Well this is a turn up for the books," said Mr Atkins. "Calls for a celebration! What d'you say, Muriel?"

"Absolutely, Atkins!" she said, picking up the telephone. "Hello, Harrods? Mrs Atkins here. I want an express delivery of twelve bottles of champagne, a side of smoked salmon, a hundredweight of caviare . . . what? *Sold out?* You've sent it all *where?* To the *nick?*"

Inspector Thumper was most surprised to see the smart party in evening dress marching up to the police station counter. "Can I help you, madam?" he asked wearily.

"We have come to be arrested," said Mrs Atkins firmly.

"Sorry madam, we're full," said Thumper, pointing in the direction of the cells, from which the sounds of riotous merriment could be heard. "We may have a vacancy next Tuesday."

"Can't you squeeze us in tonight, squire?" pleaded Mr Atkins. "I'm a really bad character. Swindling, false pretences, forgery . . ."

"And our Rolls Royce is parked on a double yellow line right outside!" added Mrs Atkins.

"Sorry madam," said Thumper smugly. "Not an arrestable offence." Mrs Atkins lost her patience. She grabbed Thumper by the collar and pulled him across the counter.

"Hit him, Atkins!"

"Sorry about this, squire," said Mr Atkins, removing Thumper's cap and bopping him lightly on the head.

"Wooley Wendy!"

The social worker plucked up her courage and timidly tweaked Superintendent Thumper's nose.

"There you are!" said Mrs Atkins. "Assaulting the police! Now are we in, or do we have to get really tough?"

"Very well, madam," said Thumper. "We'll try to squeeze you in. Move along inside there, three more coming in!"

48

By midnight the party was in full swing. Marmalade was passing round the party poopers, Whacker and Prod were telling their policemen jokes, and Superintendent Thumper with his trousers rolled up to his knees, was leading the assembled criminals in a rousing chorus of The Laughing Policeman. Then a terrible voice rang out.

"And what is the meaning of this?"

There in the doorway stood a small but very senior policeman indeed, with a huge badge on his cap, and a chest festooned with medal ribbons.

"Oh, lor!" said Superintendent Thumper. "It's Commissioner Newchap!"

"Explain yourself, Thumper!" said Commissioner Newchap in such cold steely tones that Thumper went pale.

"Well, sir," he stammered. "It's a bit complicated like. Inspector Marmalade here thought it would be a good idea like if we made the nick a bit more cosy sort of thing, and well, I s'pose things got a bit out of hand. Roll me trousers down now, shall I sir? Won't happen again, sir!"

"Indeed it will not . . . Constable Thumper!" said Commissioner Newchap.

"Blimey!" said Whacker and Prod. "'E's demoted 'im!"

"And as for you, Inspector Marmalade . . . you are dismissed from the Force!"

"Suit yourself, cock!" said Inspector Marmalade.

"Constables Whacker and Prod!" said Newchap. "Put these prisoners on bread and water!"

"Here look squire, we're not real criminals!" wailed Mr Atkins.

"I demand to see my solicitor!" shrieked Mrs Atkins.

"But I'm a social worker!" sobbed Wendy Wooley.

Commissioner Newchap smiled a cold little smile, and the iron door to the cells slammed shut.

"So long, folks!" said Marmalade. "See you on Visiting Day!"

Marmalade's Masterpiece

After they had been released from prison, Mr and Mrs Atkins went on a World Cruise, leaving Marmalade behind. While they were away, Marmalade went pony trekking in Harrods China Department, and the Atkinses were not well pleased to find a bill for £3479.60 waiting for them on their return. Still, it had been a good trip: Mr Atkins had made a lot of new business contacts, and Mrs Atkins had collected quite a few souvenirs. In fact, the living room looked quite crowded with four life-sized stuffed camels, a real gondola, and various works of art including the Venus de Milo, and a picture of a lady with a lopsided smile that Mr Atkins had slipped under his jacket while the gallery attendant was looking the other way.

"Don't suppose they'll miss her too much," he said optimistically. "After all, they've got plenty more. When the heat's died down, I'll sell her to the Sheikhs."

"Good idea, Atkins," said his wife. "Only wish you could sell Marmalade at the same time."

"Leave it out, cock," said Marmalade, who was busy with her paintbox. "I'm doing you a favour here!"

The Atkinses turned to see what sort of favour Marmalade was doing them, and what they saw made Mr Atkins go white with horror and Mrs Atkins go raspberry red with rage. Marmalade had painted a large walrus moustache on the Mona Lisa.

"Disguise, cock, see?" said Marmalade proudly.

"Oh lor!" said Mr Atkins. "How am I going to sell her to the Sheikhs now? Wipe it off at once!"

"Whatever you say, cock," said Marmalade. The wiping off was not a success. When she had finished, the Mona Lisa had a smart black beard as well as a moustache.

"S'pose I could try to pass her off as the Laughing Cavalier," said Mr Atkins, who always tried to look on the bright side. But Mrs Atkins had had enough.

"This is the end!" she cried. "This dreadful girl ruins all our hopes of happiness! Throw her out of the window, it's the only way!"

"Right you are, Muriel, whatever you say," said Mr Atkins.

The Atkinses were busy chasing Marmalade under the cocktail cabinet and up and down the camels' humps when Wendy Wooley arrived.

"I say! Gosh! Super!" she cried. "What is it? Charades? Psychodrama? Can I join in?"

"It's called murder, Miss Wooley, and you certainly can!" growled Marmalade's mother through gritted teeth.

"Oh, I just love your sense of humour, Mrs Atkins. You *are* joking, aren't you?"

"No, I am not joking! Look what she's done!"

Wendy Wooley looked. "Oh! I see! Gosh! Well! Wow!"

Then she looked again.

"Er . . . *ace!*"

"*Ace?*" gasped Mr and Mrs Atkins.

"Yes," said Wendy defiantly. "Absolutely ace! Jolly original and creative!"

"Atkins," said Marmalade's mother. "Wooley Wendy has flipped. Throw her out of the window too!"

"No, no, Mrs Atkins, just stop and think for a moment. Every problem is an opportunity in disguise! By this little act of girlish vandalism, Marmalade is telling us about her frustrated artistic talents! This must be the key to all her problems! She's a frustrated genius!"

"Just what I always thought, cock," said Marmalade.

"Marmalade," said Wendy Wooley. "I'm going to enrol you in Art School! And not just any old Art School! I'm going to sign you up with the greatest genius of all . . . Salvador Barmi himself!"

The Salvador Barmi School of Art was a dark and dusty sort of place. The hight vaulted ceilings were full of bats and cobwebs, and strange sounds like moans and groans echoed down the long dim corridors. Marmalade Atkins felt strangely small and shy as she stood alone in the vast Drawing Studio, surrounded by huge and ancient canvases, towering statues of ancient warriors, and glass cases full of stuffed eagles, vultures, badgers, stoats, and foxes. It wasn't Marmalade's idea of an Art School and she didn't like the look of it a bit.

Then suddenly a figure emerged from the shadows, dressed in shiny black leather trousers and a cloak of brilliant dragonfly blue. But the most amazing thing about this person was his moustache, which was curled into such intricate shapes that it looked as if its owner was peering through a wrought iron gate. It was Professor Salvador Barmi himself!

"I am the great Salvador Barmi," he hissed, "and I detest the free and easy ways of the younger generation!" Marmalade was determined to stick up for herself.

"My name is Marmalade Atkins and I muck about," she said.

Salvador Barmi glared at her with his piercing blue eyes and pinged the end of his moustache like a tuning fork.

"So I understand. But there is no mucking about in my

school! Here the students do what they are told, they paint masterpieces by numbers and make lots and lots of money for Salvador Barmi! And that is what you will do too! Have you any questions?"

"Yes, cock," said Marmalade. "Is that a moustache, or are you peering through a wrought iron gate?"

But Marmalade Atkins soon found out that Salvador Barmi's studio was more like a factory than an Art School. The students (Barmi called them his Miserable Slaves of Art) were the saddest looking people that Marmalade had ever seen. They all wore long dingy brown smocks and scruffy brown carpet slippers, and when the bell rang they shuffled to their places, heads hung low, without a word or a laugh. They were all older than Marmalade, and two of them had beards down to their knees.

"Morning mates!" said Marmalade chirpily. "When's Rag Day? When does the mucking about start?"

Not a word from the Miserable Slaves of Art. Salvador Barmi rang another bell and they all started painting Masterpieces by Numbers. Each easel had a big canvas, all marked out in numbers where the different colours were to go, and each Miserable Slave of Art had to finish ten masterpieces a day. Marmalade watched the brushes flashing in and out of the little paint-pots and filling in the little squares on the canvas, all in time to the ticking of Salvador Barmi's great clock on the wall (the hands looked remarkably like moustaches).

"Here cock," said Marmalade. "What do I do?"

"What do you do, miserable worm? You can draw me a banana!"

He tossed a long brown smock over Marmalade's head and sat her down to work on a canvas with a huge outline of a banana on it. On the outline was written: BANANA.

53

NUMBER ONE: YELLOW.

"This is a bit boring, isn't it?" said Marmalade.

"It is the rule of the School of Barmi. Everybody begins with a banana. Strive hard, you Miserable Slaves of Art! Today the great Professor Blenkinsop from the Royal Gallery of Old-fashioned Painting is coming to visit us and inspect your feeble efforts. Strive hard, strive hard!"

And Salvador Barmi swept out to his private room to polish up his moustache for the Professor's visit. Today was to be a great day. Salvador Barmi intended to sell all his students' paintings to the Royal Gallery of Old-fashioned Painting and retire to Torremolinos on the proceeds!

Back in the studio, the Miserable Slaves of Art were toiling away. Not a sound could be heard but the ticking of the moustache clock and the swishing of the brushes. Marmalade couldn't stand it.

"Here," she said. "Fellow Slaves of Art! Is this all we do, then?"

"This is all we do, Marmalade Atkins," said the Miserable Slaves of Art.

Marmalade added a big curly moustache to her banana, and gave it a pair of black shiny trousers like Salvador Barmi's.

"Much better," said Marmalade Atkins. She looked at the clock. The big moustache was pointing to the six and the little moustache was halfway between the ten and the eleven.

"Half past ten," said Marmalade. "It must be playtime."

"There is no playtime at the Barmi School of Art," said the Miserable Slaves. "Only work, work, work."

"Well, I always have me playtime," said Marmalade. "When d'you eat your crisps? When d'you whiz about on the old roller skates? When d'you muck about, eh?"

No answer from the miserable slaves. Tick, tick, tick, went the clock. Swish, swish, swish, went the brushes. Marmalade got out her crisps and whizzed about on her roller skates, but nobody else joined in.

Then Salvador Barmi strode into the studio to inspect the masterpieces. He prowled around the easels pinging his moustache and striking fear into the hearts of the Miserable Slaves of Art. And then he came to Marmalade's banana.

"And what is this?" he roared.

"Modern Art," said Marmalade. "Don't you like it?"

"Modern Art!" screamed Barmi. "I loathe and detest it! Into the dustbin with Modern Art!"

He hurled Marmalade's masterpiece into the dustbin. "And into the dustbin with Marmalade Atkins!" This was not so easy. Marmalade Atkins was very nippy on her skates, and the chase lasted a long time. Marmalade didn't really mean to skate through three pots of paint; and she didn't really mean to knock three masterpieces flat on the floor; and she didn't really mean to skate all over them, leaving shiny trails of red and yellow paint that crossed and recrossed the paintings like shiny wet knitting. But that was what she did. Salvador Barmi made a last desperate lunge, slipped in the pool of yellow paint, and sat down in it, his leather trousers making a satisfying squelching sound.

"Marmalade Atkins," he whispered savagely. "You are expelled!"

"See your point, cock," said Marmalade reasonably. "But I'll be back. Modern Art will triumph in the end!"

As she was skating down the road outside, she nearly bumped into a very small and distinguished looking gentleman, with a big black hat, a big black cloak, and a big black beard.

"Can you direct me to the Salvador Barmi School of Art,

young lady?" said the very small gentleman.

"Easy," said Marmalade. "You're not that Professor Blenkinsop geezer, are you?"

"Indeed I am, young lady. I have come to inspect the students' work."

"Ah," said Marmalade, thinking quickly. "Mr Barmi sends his apologies, but the exhibition won't be ready till this afternoon."

"This is most irregular," said Professor Blenkinsop.

"Mr Barmi says please would you go and have a slap-up lunch at the Ritz Hotel, and of course he'll pay the bill."

"Ah! That's more like it!" said Professor Blenkinsop, who liked a good blow-out as much as you or I. "Tell Mr Barmi that I shall return at three precisely!"

And Professor Blenkinsop waddled off to the Ritz, while Marmalade skated off to the Joke and Fancy Dress shop.

Salvador Barmi and the Miserable Slaves had just managed to clear up the worst of the mess when they heard three loud knocks on the door, and a very small figure in a big black hat, a big black cloak, and a big black bushy beard walked into the studio.

"Ah, Professor Blenkinsop!" cried Barmi, fawning and wriggling and rubbing his hands in a way that was quite revolting. "What a delightful surprise! Welcome to my humble school!"

"Never mind that, Barmi," said Marmalade through a mass of black whiskers. "I'm a busy man. Let's have a butchers at the jolly old works of art. If I like what I see, I've got half a million smackeroos of public money to spend!"

"Half a million!" squealed Barmi, cringing and wriggling with delight. "Come this way, Professor, come this way!" And he led Marmalade to the Exhibition Room, which was full of the Masterpieces by Numbers painted by

57

the Miserable Slaves.

"Boring, boring," said Marmalade.

"Yes indeed, professor, very boring," said Barmi, "I quite agree, you see I show you the worst first . . ." He chewed his moustache with anxiety. What had gone wrong?

"Rubbish!" said Marmalade. "Old-fashioned rubbish, the lot of it!"

"Yes indeed," moaned Barmi, old-fashioned rubbish, just what I think myself, h dear, oh dear, he doesn't like it, what am I going to do?"

"Where's all the Modern Art?" said Marmalade.

"Modern Art!" gasped Barmi. "I loathe and detest . . . you said *modern* art?"

"Yes, we've gone all modern at the Royal Gallery," said Marmalade. "Chucking out all the old-fashioned rubbish." Out of the corner of her eye she could see her roller skated painting, covered with a big white sheet.

"What's that there?"

"Ah, no, professor, don't look at that, it's just rubbish, a disaster, not for your eyes . . ."

Marmalade whipped the sheet off.

"Magnificent!" she said.

"Yes, it is magnificent, isn't it?" said Barmi, wondering if he had gone mad.

"A great work of modern art!" said the fake professor. "Where is the student who created this masterpiece?"

"Oh, she's just popped out for a minute!" said Barmi desperately. "But . . . but all my students can paint like this!"

"Indeed?" said Marmalade. "Let me see."

"Well, er, professor, the Modern Art Exhibition is not quite ready, if the great and famous professor would care to come back to Open Day this afternoon he will see a Modern Art Exhibition such as he has never seen before!"

"All right, Barmi, I'll believe you," said Marmalade. "I'm off to the Ritz now, but I'll be back at three precisely!"

After he had moaned and groaned and kicked the school cat and twanged his moustache so hard it brought tears to his eyes, Salvador Barmi pulled himself together and rushed out to buy twenty seven pairs of roller skates. The Miserable Slaves strapped them on, sloshed them through the paint, and had more fun than they'd ever had in their sad old lives skating madly about over Salvador Barmi's old-fashioned masterpieces. And by three o'clock the Modern Art Exhibition was ready.

Lots of posh and arty people came to Salvador Barmi's Open Day, including Mr and Mrs Atkins and Wendy Wooley, and they all stared at the exhibition in bewilderment.

"Oh, gosh, wow," said Wendy Wooley. "I never thought it would be so . . . strange! It really is mega-modern, isn't it?"

"Certainly is," said Mr Atkins. "Cor, look at that one, Muriel. Looks as if someone's roller skated all over it then sat down in a pool of paint ar, ar, ar!"

"Oh, shut up Atkins and don't show your ignorance!" hissed Marmalade's mother.

Salvador Barmi twanged his moustache for attention. "Ladies and gentlemen, welcome to the Open Day of the New Improved Salvador Barmi School of Modern Art!"

Just as everyone stopped clapping, the door opened and the real Professor Blenkinsop waddled in, burping quietly into his beard. He had rather overdone it at the Ritz and was not in the best of moods.

"Ah, Professor!" cried Barmi. "You see I keep my word! Look! Half a million pounds worth of masterpieces!"

Professor Blenkinsop stared around him in amazement

and disgust. "I never saw such rubbish in my life, Barmi!" he growled. "Do you try to make a fool of the world's greatest art expert? Good afternoon to you."

"No! Wait! Wait!" screamed Barmi, wondering what could have gone wrong this time. "Ah! I know what the matter is! It's not modern enough, is it? Well, Salvador Barmi can be more modern than that! Look! Action painting!" And he picked up a big can of paint and sloshed it all over one of the canvases. Unfortunately some of the paint went over Mrs Atkins's new fur coat.

"Don't you Modern Art me, my man," she said grimly, and she picked up another can of paint and sloshed it all over Salvador Barmi, who staggered backwards straight through one of the largest canvases.

"You see, professor!" he moaned in desperation, sticking his head out through the hole, his moustache dripping orange paint. "Living sculpture!"

"The man's gone mad!" said the professor. "Stop him, someone!"

"I know what you mean!" screamed Barmi. "Still not modern enough! Wait! Wait! I jump in the paint! I roll on the canvas! Salvador Barmi, the human paintbrush! Instant masterpiece!"

"Arrest this madman!" shouted Professor Blenkinsop, who was becoming seriously alarmed.

"Gosh, wow, I really think he's flipped!" said Wendy Wooley, and she blew her special emergency Social Worker's Whistle. Two men in white coats rushed in and seized Professor Blenkinsop.

"No, not him, him!" cried Wendy, and the two men dropped Professor Blenkinsop and went after Salvador Barmi.

"Wait! Wait!" yelled Barmi. "I saw off my leg and paint with the soggy end! For half a million I do anything!" The men in white coats grabbed him and began to carry him out.

"Wait! Wait! I'm not mad! I'm Barmi!"

"Poor fellow. Poor fellow," said Professor Blenkinsop, shaking his head sadly. Just then Marmalade appeared in the doorway, still dressed in her disguise.

"Aaargh! I'm seeing double!" shrieked Salvador Barmi. "I *am* mad! Take me away!" And then the men in white coats bundled him into a white van and took him away to a home for mad professors, where he lived quite happily ever after.

"Terrible business," said Professor Blenkinsop to Marmalade.

"Yes, indeed," said Marmalade. "Shocking."

"You look like an art expert to me," said Professor Blenkinsop.

"Certainly am," said Marmalade. "Professor Marmalade from Bangkok."

"Nothing but rubbish here, Professor Marmalade."

"Indeed, Professor Blenkinsop. Very sad. Except for one rather jolly little piece. I've just picked it up for a tenner," said Marmalade.

"May I see?" said Professor Blenkinsop. And Marmalade showed him her picture of the moustachioed banana.

"It's an early Atkins, you know," she said, fluffing up her beard.

"Ah, yes, of course," said Professor Blenkinsop. Very fine. You wouldn't consider parting with it, I suppose?"

"It's yours for twelve fifty and tea at the Ritz," said Marmalade.

"Done!" said Professor Blenkinsop. "Shall we go, Professor Marmalade?"

"After you, Professor Blenkinsop!"

The Atkinses and Wendy Wooley watched the two little figures waddling out in their black hats and cloaks.

"That's funny," said Wendy after a while. "I wonder what happened to Marmalade?"

61

Marmalade at the Working Men's Club

Dr Glenfiddick was getting worried about Wendy Wooley. She had taken to coming to work in leg-warmers and calling him *cock* again, and talking about Sisterhood and a place called Greenham Common he had never heard of. She was not the nice quiet respectful Miss Wooley she used to be, and Dr Glenfiddick was determined to do something about it. He was also going to have to do something about Marmalade Atkins again. Since her parents had been released from jail, she was not *In Care* any more, but she was still at large; she was still putting herself about, and the thought of this made Dr Glenfiddick very uneasy.

"Why not let her have her fun?" suggested Wendy Wooley. "After all, we're only young once!"

"Something has come over you, Miss Wooley," said Dr Glenfiddick. "We do not go in for Fun in the Social Services. We go in for Problems. Marmalade Atkins is a Problem, and you are becoming a Problem too. Let us go and visit the Atkinses."

They found the Atkinses at home; and things were quite peaceful, for an ordinary afternoon in the Atkins house. Marmalade was practising darts. She did this by throwing them at the Mona Lisa, which was Mrs Atkins's favourite picture. Marmalade was very good at darts, and could hit the Mona Lisa on the nose five times running. Mrs Atkins did not approve of this.

"Atkins!" she shrieked. "Make her stop!"

"Give it a rest, Marmalade," said Mr Atkins.

Marmalade didn't stop.

"No good, Muriel," said Mr Atkins, turning to the racing page of the newspaper. "She doesn't want to stop."

"Atkins, you're pathetic! Call yourself a man! Assert yourself!"

"Now, look here, Marmalade," said Mr Atkins forcefully. "If you don't stop, I'm . . . I'm . . . I'm off for a pint down the Working Men's Club."

"Coward! Sissy!" yelled Mrs Atkins, and knocked him down with a large cushion.

"Go it, Mum! Up the women!" said Marmalade.

It was then that Wendy Wooley and Dr Glenfiddick arrived.

"Ah, morning, squire," said Mr Atkins, on his hands and knees. "I was just thinking of crawling down to the Working Men's Club for a pint, fancy coming?"

"Yes, indeed, Mr Atkins," said Dr Glenfiddick. "But first we have to deal with our womenfolk!"

"Yes, well, I just dealt with mine," said Mr Atkins. "She won't forget that hiding in a hurry."

Mrs Atkins gave him a whack with the teacosy, and he collapsed with a groan to the carpet.

"So," said Dr Glenfiddick. "Things have come to a pretty pass."

"Me and my mum, we put ourselves about," said Marmalade proudly.

"Not any more you don't," said Dr Glenfiddick.

"I *beg* your pardon?" said Mrs Atkins, reaching for the teacosy again.

"I was referring to your daughter!" said Glenfiddick hastily.

"Ah, I see," said Mrs Atkins. "That's all right then, Dr Drambuie."

63

"Here, leave it out, Mum!" said Marmalade. "You're letting down the Women's Movement!"

"Yes, that's jolly well right!" said Wendy Wooley. "Sometimes I jolly well feel like putting myself about as well, so there!"

"Right!" said Glenfiddick. "This nonsense has gone quite far enough. As Senior Officer in the Social Services I am taking over this case!" (He didn't notice that Marmalade was tying his shoelaces together). "And my ruling is that this little delinquent needs a different sort of Work Experience, something hard and boring!"

"Drilling holes in roads, cock?" said Marmalade.

"No! Sweeping floors in the Working Men's Club!" And you, Miss Wooley, *you* are going to be the *barmaid*! Come on, Atkins, let's go for that pint!"

Dr Glenfiddick took one manful stride towards the door and fell flat on his face.

"Oh, I do love a man who stands up for himself!" said Mrs Atkins.

Life was grim for Marmalade and Wendy when they started work in the Tufftown Working Men's club. Marmalade found herself the Lowest of the Low again, toiling away from morning till night sweeping up crisp packets, betting slips and fag ends, while all around her the Working Men laughed and sang and drank beer and told jokes and played darts. Marmalade would have liked to do some of those things too, particularly the darts, but the Working Men would have none of that. Skivvies were there to skivvy, in their opinion, and they took not the least bit of notice of her.

It was no more fun for Wendy Wooley either, pulling pints till her arm ached, wiping down the greasy tables, and enduring the vulgar jokes. She was beginning to feel fed up with the whole thing. But she was determined to stick it out with Marmalade, and show Dr Glenfiddick how women and girls could stand together against the men. But it was a hard life.

"Get 'em in!" shouted the Working Men. "Get 'em in . . . Your shout . . . By, that's a good pint . . . By, never touched the sides . . . Have you been down the labour . . . Have you got your giro . . . By, that's a good pint . . . How about a game of arrows?"

That was how the Working Men went on, hour after hour, and when they had drunk their pints of beer and told their jokes, they all went over to the dartboard for a game of arrows.

The best players in the club were called Plump Percy, Thin Stanley and Medium Maurice. Marmalade took her broom over to the dartboard to watch them playing. Plump Percy was the best of them, but Marmalade didn't think he was all that good. She doubted whether he could get the Mona Lisa on the nose five times in a row. So when Plump Percy had won his game, finishing on the double twenty as all the flashy players do, she said:

"Give us a go, cock. I can do that!"

The three Working Men turned and stared.

"You hear a voice then, Stan?" said Plump Percy.

"Thought I heard a mouse squeak," said Thin Stanley.

"Thought I heard a pip squeak," said Medium Maurice.

"Ar, Ar, Ar!" went all the Working Men.

"You. Shrimp. Out of the road," said Plump Percy. "Men's work, this is."

"But I like darts," said Marmalade. Thin Stanley and Medium Maurice picked Marmalade up.

"Throw her out the window, Perce?"

"Stuff her in the dustbin, Perce?"

"Hey, you!" shouted Wendy Wooley from the bar. "Don't you dare treat my little client like that!"

65

Stanley and Maurice dropped Marmalade and stared over at Wendy Wooley.

"Hark at that, Perce," said Thin Stanley.

"Hark at that new barmaid," said Medium Maurice.

"Let's have a pint, boys," said Plump Percy.

The Working Men strode over to the bar and propped themselves up on their mighty elbows.

"Pint of Strong, duck!"

"Pint of Hard, duck!"

"Pint of Heavy, duck!"

"I am not a duck, gentlemen!" said Wendy Wooley bravely. "I am a woman!"

"Could have fooled us, duck, ar, ar, ar!"

"Good one that, Perce, ar, ar, ar!"

"How dare you?" said Wendy Wooley crossly.

"And what's all this, lads?" said Perce. "What's she wearing?" All the Working Men peered at Wendy's denim dungarees and went tut, tut, tut.

"Bib and brace behind the bar, lads, that's not right!" said Plump Percy. "Doesn't show respect for the Working Man! Ought to be a blouse, eh? Aye, lads, worr!"

"I'll choose my own clothes, thank you very much, gentlemen!" said Wendy.

"That's where you're wrong, duck, matter for the committee this!" said Plump Percy.

"Who's the committee?" said Wendy Wooley.

"We are, duck! Barmaids in blouses, all those in favour?" Plump Percy, Medium Maurice and Thin Stanley all put their hands up.

"Against?" Marmalade and Wendy put their hands up.

"Only members vote, duck. Motion carried!"

That evening, the Tufftown Working Men's Club was even fuller than it had been in the afternoon. Wendy Wooley,

66

feeling cross and embarrassed in her new low-cut blouse, was pulling pints fit to bust, and Marmalade was sweeping up a pile of rubbish as high as her head. Mr Atkins and Dr Glenfiddick leaned on the bar feeling like big strong Working Men.

"Well squire," said Mr Atkins. "I'd never have believed it."

"Sometimes a man's got to do what a man's got to do," said Dr Glenfiddick solemnly. "Pint of Strong, Miss Wooley!"

"Pint of Heavy here, duck," said Mr Atkins.

"Beastly male chauvinists," muttered Wendy Wooley.

"Ar, ar, ar nice blouse eh worr!" chortled Dr Glenfiddick and Mr Atkins.

Late that night, when all the Working Men had gone home, Marmalade sat on top of the huge pile of rubbish watching Wendy Wooley dry the last of the glasses.

"Oh, it's so humiliating, Marmalade," said Wendy Wooley. "We are slaves in a world of men!"

"Yeah," said Marmalade. "We are. At the moment. Here, wait a minute. I've got an idea. If you can't beat 'em join 'em!"

"Marmalade! Whatever do you mean?"

The following morning, Plump Percy, Medium Maurice and Thin Stanley were just downing the first pints of the day when they were surprised to see a very small figure marching purposefully towards the bar. The small figure was dressed in a blue serge suit, a shirt without a collar, and a big cloth cap. But the most remarkable thing about this person was the huge black moustache, one of the biggest ever seen in the Tufftown Working Men's Club.

"Morning, lads," said Marmalade. "I'm a new member. Moustache Atkins is the name, and darts is the game!"

"Hey, lads!" said Plump Percy. "They're letting in

midgets now!"

"What'll you drink, Shorty?" said Thin Stanley.

"Pint of pop," said Marmalade.

"Lads," said Plump Percy, "we are drinking with a softy!"

"I may be short," said Marmalade. "But I'm not soft. I'm hard. Dead hard. So watch it."

"Oh, yeah?" sneered Plump Percy.

"Yeah," said Marmalade. "For example, I can make the beer jump out of your glass without even touching it!"

"Oh yeah?"

"Yeah. Get a bit closer . . . watch the beer. Don't take your eyes off it . . ."

Suddenly Marmalade picked up the glass and threw the beer all over Plump Percy's head.

"Oh, wow, super, ace, serves him right!" said Wendy Wooley, then clapped her hand over her mouth. There was a short ominous silence.

"Shorty, this means war," said Plump Percy. "Name your weapons."

"Arrows, cock," said Mr Moustache Atkins. "On the ocky, ten o'clock tonight!"

By ten o'clock that night a great crowd had gathered at the Tufftown Working Men's club, as the word had got round about the great challenge match between Plump Percy and the mystery midget. There was even a television team there to record the climax of the match, because Plump Percy was a famous player who had never been beaten in his own club.

"And you've joined us at the very climax," said the commentator. "Both men in with a chance now. Plump Percy, the Southern Area Champion, Mr Beergut himself, to throw first, needing sixty-seven to finish!"

Plump Percy stepped on to the groaning boards of the stage, drained a pint of beer to polite applause, then picked

68

up his darts and threw the first one.

"Seven . . ." said the commentator . . . "and a twenty . . . double twenty needed to finish!"

Plump Percy took careful aim and threw, then turned away in rage as his dart went just the wrong side of the wire and landed in the double one. The great crowd gasped and groaned.

"And now it's the turn of Mr Moustache the Mystery Midget, needing only double top to beat the Southern Area Champion!"

Marmalade drained her pop with a gurgle and took aim, pretending that the double top was the Mona Lisa's nose.

"And the midget's hit the digit!" shouted the commentator. Marmalade had won!

Next day in the club, Mr Moustache Atkins was the most popular member. Everyone wanted to buy bottles of pop and packets of crisps and bubblegum for the new champion of the Southern Area. Everyone except Plump Percy, who was sulking on his own in a corner.

"Fat Freddy next," said Mr Moustache Atkins. "I'm going to challenge him for the English championship!"

"You'll never beat Fat Freddy!" snarled Plump Percy, pulling the feathers out of his darts in frustration.

"Percy's sulking ar, ar, ar!" said Thin Stanley. "Lost 'is trophy ar, ar, ar!"

Then the club fell silent as an enormously fat man walked in. He was so fat that Wendy Wooley had to unlock both sides of the double doors before he could get through them.

"It's Fat Freddy!" gasped the Working Men.

Fat Freddy waddled up to the bar and fixed Marmalade a steely gaze. "Heard you play a crafty game of arrows, Mr Moustache Atkins," he said.

"Yes, that's right, cock, I bung 'em about a bit," said

Marmalade modestly.

"Fancy a game tonight with the champion?" said Fat Freddy.

"Don't mind if I do," said Marmalade.

"Ten o'clock tonight, on the ocky," said Fat Freddy and walked out of the club, with all the Working Men chasing after him to get his autograph.

That evening, all the television cameras were there again to see the sensational Mr Moustache Atkins in his challenge for the English Championship. Mr Atkins and Dr Glenfiddick were there as well, and Wendy Wooley's arms were working like pistons pulling pints for the vast crowd.

"Here we are again at the Tufftown Working Men's Club," said the commentator, "and the sensation of the nation is that Fat Freddy Fanshaw the all-England Champion is fighting for his life against Mr Moustache, the mystery midget! And it's Fat Freddy to finish needing eighty eight!"

Fat Freddy stepped up, popped a cream bun as big as a football in his mouth, and took careful aim.

"Eighty eight required," said the Commentator. "There's the eight. There's the double top. Only another double top required!" Fat Freddy turned, smiled a nasty smile at Marmalade, and popped another huge cream bun in his mouth to steady his aim. Marmalade popped her bubblegum, and Fat Freddy threw!

"Oh, and it's just the wrong side of the wire, he's hit the double five, he won't be pleased with that one!" cried the commentator. Fat Freddy was not well pleased. He stamped his foot so hard it went right through the stage, and then he squashed two cream buns in the commentator's face.

"No, I could tell he was disappointed there," said the commentator indistinctly. "And now it's Mr Moustache. Only forty required to take Fat Freddy's England Crown!"

Marmalade stepped up to the board and winked at Wendy Wooley. Then she threw one dart. Straight into the double twenty!

"And the midget's hit the digit again!" yelled the commentator. "We have a new champion here tonight!"

"Good old Marmalade!" shouted Wendy Wooley, forgetting that Marmalade's disguise was supposed to be a secret. She clapped her hand over her mouth and looked round nervously, but no one seemed to have noticed, she thought. But she was wrong. Dr Glenfiddick had.

"She's got to be taught a lesson!" said Dr Glenfiddick in the bar next day.

Well, don't expect any help from me, duck," said Wendy Wooley. "I'm only the barmaid!"

Suddenly Glenfiddick had an idea. "There's only one man who can beat the Moustache now!" he shouted. Everyone in the club turned round.

"No one can beat Mr Moustache Atkins!" said the Working Men.

"Aberdeen Angus can," said Dr Glenfiddick.

"Aberdeen Angus? Never heard of him!" said Plump Percy.

"You will, Percy, you will," said Dr Glenfiddick.

"And it's another sensational night at the Tufftown Working Men's Club!" said the commentator. "A challenge from the North. Now nobody knows much about this Aberdeen Angus, except that he always plays with his own dartboard. But he's got the weight for it, and here he comes now!"

If you have ever watched darts on TV you will know that most of the best players are fat men, and some of them are very fat indeed. In fact a lot of people say that the fatter you are, the better you will be at darts. If those people are right, then Aberdeen Angus was quite a darts player. He looked like a big red balloon. Not the sort you get at parties, but the sort you go round the world in eighty days with. And on top of his head was an enormous tam-o-shanter. He had a very whiskery face, and he reminded Marmalade of someone. In fact, if he hadn't been so immensely fat, and if he hadn't had so many whiskers, he would have reminded her of . . . but no. That was impossible. One thing was certain, he was a wonderful darts player, and Marmalade was losing for the first time in her life.

Aberdeen Angus waddled up to the stage, which had been specially strengthened for the occasion. He had a very unusual throwing action. He tossed each dart high into the air, but then it looped and wiggled and homed in straight for the treble twenty.

"One hundred and eighty!" said the commentator. Aberdeen Angus grinned round at the crowd, took his darts out of the board, and put them on his baccy tin. Marmalade watched. There was something strange about the way they stood up straight on the metal, as if they were magnetised. And suddenly she realised Aberdeen Angus's secret.

"Mr Moustache to throw, and a worried wee man he is tonight!" said the commentator.

Marmalade threw her darts. One in the treble twenty, one in the double twenty, but the third was just an ordinary twenty.

"One hundred and twenty!" said the commentator. Marmalade took her darts and scuttled off into the wings.

"And here's Aberdeen Angus wanting just the double top to finish, it's just a formality now, I don't see how Mr Moustache can do anything to keep his title . . ."

Marmalade rushed back, and what she held in her hands made Aberdeen Angus turn pale. It was a giant magnet.

Aberdeen Angus threw his first dart. It looped high in the air as before, but instead of whizzing into the treble

72

twenty, it changed direction, and flew off sideways straight on to Marmalade's magnet, where it stuck fast.

All the Working Men gasped at Angus's sudden lack of form, but nobody knew the reason, except for Marmalade. Aberdeen Angus's darts were magnetised, and that was why he always used his own dartboard! And now it was Marmalade's turn to throw again.

"Mr Moustache, needing one hundred and seventy! He'll never finish from here!" said the commentator.

Marmalade threw the first dart.

"Sixty!"

Marmalade threw the second dart.

"Sixty again, one hundred and twenty, will he go for the bullseye to finish?"

Marmalade took aim, the dart flew threw the air . . .

"One hundred and seventy! Game and match to Mr Moustache Atkins! And what's he doing now? Has he gone mad? He's attacking his opponent with a dart!"

To the amazement of the Working Men, Marmalade stuck the point of the dart in Aberdeen Angus's backside. There was an ear-splitting hiss and a great rush of air. Aberdeen Angus was deflating! Marmalade pulled off his tam and his whiskers, and there, exposed for all to see, was . . . Dr Glenfiddick!

"You rotten old cheat!" said Marmalade.

"I only did it for the best! It was only to teach her a lesson!" gabbled Glenfiddick.

"Get him, lads!" roared Plump Percy. And as the Working Men of Tufftown chased Glenfiddick away into the night, Marmalade strolled across to the bar.

"Fancy a nice quiet game, Wendy? Just us girls?"

"Why, Marmalade!" said Wendy Wooley pulling on her dungarees, "what a nice idea!"

And that was how Darts For Women got started.

Airplane Atkins

Dr Glenfiddick, the head of the Social Services, was a famous psychologist, but like some other famous psychologists, he had his soppy side. As he sat at his desk fiddling with his paperclips, he found himself thinking more and more about Wendy Wooley. Her Work Experience Scheme had been quite a success, but it was more than that. People said that she looked like a mad sheep, but Dr Glenfiddick had a soft spot for sheep. He had once had a pet sheep called Deirdre, and he began to think that he would like to make a pet of Wendy Wooley. So when she breezed into his office one morning in her new spotty dungarees and her *Marmalade Rules OK* badge, he didn't make any sarcastic remarks at all.

"Ah, Miss Wooley," he said politely. "How pretty you're looking today!"

"Never mind that," said Wendy briskly. "I've got a new idea for Marmalade!"

"Oh, er . . . good," said Dr Glenfiddick warily.

"It involves *travel*," said Wendy.

"Travel . . . far away?" asked Glenfiddick hopefully.

"Travel *very* far away!"

Dr Glenfiddick sighed. If only it could come true! With Marmalade on the other side of the world, perhaps he and his favourite social worker could bring each other happiness!

"Perhaps, Miss Wooley, in that case," he murmured, "we might be alone together. A little Highland croft, say.

Scotch pancakes by the gas fire? I could sing you my songs of Bonnie Scotland. I-I-och, why not admit it? I'm in love with you, Miss Wooley!"

"Gosh! Wow! Love!" said Wendy. "That's a bit claggy. I mean, well, awfully flattered, but I'm just not *into* being soppy just now, life's just too full and exciting and mega-meaningful, gosh is that the time, must dash!"

And she breezed out of the office without even telling him what the new plan was, and went straight to the Atkinses.

"Hello, folks, it's Wendy!" she called, as she roller skated into the living room. She had only just bought the roller skates, a beautiful spotted pair to match her new dungarees, and she wasn't very good at controlling them yet. With a high bleat, like a startled sheep, she tripped over the edge of the carpet, somersaulted over the coffee table, and landed neatly on the sofa between Mr and Mrs Atkins.

"Wow!" she gasped. "This is the life, eh?"

"Good afternoon, Miss Wooley," said Mrs Atkins wearily. "What a charming outfit, have they got a sale on at Mother-care?"

"Gosh, you are witty, Mrs Atkins! No, actually, this is my way of showing my client I'm on her side! And I am! I've learnt so much from Marmalade! I'm with her all the way now! The sky's the limit, hint, hint! We're really going to take off now, nudge, nudge! Get it?"

Mr and Mrs Atkins looked at each other blearily.

"Flipped," said Mrs Atkins.

"Gone potty," said Mr Atkins.

"Marmalade!" called Wendy Wooley.

"You called, cock?" said Marmalade, entering through the window.

"You're going to love this," said Wendy Wooley. "I've got a super new job for you! You're going to learn to be an air hostess — and I'm going to help to train you!"

One week later, Marmalade Atkins found herself standing in the aisle of a huge jumbo jet. She had a silly pink uniform with a badge on it, and a silly pink hat on her head, and a fierce scowl on her face.

"This is barmy, cock," she said to Wendy Wooley. "This isn't a proper plane. And look at all these so-called passengers! How can I put meself about with this lot?"

Marmalade was right about the passengers. They weren't real people at all. The seats were full of plastic dummies of businessmen, mothers, fathers, nice little boys and nice little girls, penguins, nuns, and babies. They were all beaming at Marmalade with their blank plastic smiles.

"Marmalade, I *explained*," said Wendy Wooley. "It's a *training* plane. To *practise* on. And when you've passed your course, you'll be able to have a go with *real* people."

"Well, look, cock," said Marmalade. "I don't really want to be an air hostess anyway. I want to be a pilot!"

"I know! I know! But we've all got to start somewhere! I just know you're going to be an *ace* air hostess, and that's the first step on the ladder! You can't really expect to fly jumbo jets on your own! Well, not just yet, anyway!"

"You want a bet?" said Marmalade.

"Gosh, I love your confidence! But first things first. It's time to see if you've remembered your drill. Off you go."

"Oh, all right, cock, just to please you," said Marmalade. She screwed her face up into a soppy smile, and spoke to the dummies in her best soppy Wendy Wooley voice:

"Good morning ladies and gentlemen, boys and girls, welcome to our flight. Please ensure that your seat belts are securely fastened. No smoking, no spitting, no fighting, and no mucking about until the itty bitty lights go out. My name is Marmalade and I'm here to make your flight a happy one!"

"Super! said Wendy Wooley. "Now the safety drill."

"Now we'll demonstrate the safety drill!" gushed Marmalade. "Under your seats you will find a trendy little life-jacket!"

Wendy Wooley got one out and held it up to show the dummies, who smiled at it with their blank plastic faces.

"You put it over your head like this!" said Marmalade, and Wendy Wooley demonstrated.

"And then you put the strings round the back and tie them at the front like this!" said Marmalade. Wendy tied the strings obediently.

"There!" said Marmalade. "That wasn't very hard, was it? And when you want to blow it up, you pull the little cord like this!"

"No! No!" shrieked Wendy Wooley. Marmalade pulled the little cord, and the lifejacket inflated. Marmalade pulled the cord again, and the lifejacket inflated even more. It looked like a giant balloon. Wendy Wooley floated slowly upwards to the roof of the plane, where she bobbed and dangled helplessly.

Marmalade pushed a button on the wall, and the cabin door swung open. Then she took the microphone and spoke into it.

"OK, folks! Boarding through Gate Number Three! All aboard for the special cut-price bargain flight of the year. Take your seats and stand by for blast off!"

To Miss Wooley's amazement, a whole lot of real people came up the gangway and started to fill up the seats left vacant by the dummies. There were real Arabs, real businessmen, real nuns, and last but not least, Mr and Mrs Atkins, waving their bottles of duty-free.

"Marmalade! What's happening?" cried Wendy Wooley.

"Bottoms up, Miss Wooley," shouted Mr Atkins cheerily.

"They certainly are!" said Marmalade.

"Take your seats, ladies and gents, and prepare for

takeoff . . . and it looks like it's going to be a pretty bumpy ride! Oh, borrow your hatpin, Mum?"

She took a large pin out of her mother's mink hat and punctured Wendy's lifejacket, and the gallant social worker floated gracefully down to the floor.

"Wow, gosh, super bit of role play," she said. "But you *are* joking aren't you? I mean, this can't *really* be a *real* flight . . . er . . . can it?"

"Certainly, cock," said Marmalade. "Met the pilot this morning. Funny sort of geezer, name of Jitters."

Wendy Wooley put her hands over her eyes. "Oh, no!" she said. "Not Captain Jitters!"

Up ahead in the cockpit, Captain Jitters was climbing into his seat. He was a thin, twitchy, excitable sort of man, with wild staring eyes. He had only just returned from a long period of sickleave, and he couldn't quite remember what all the little dials were for. Still, it would probably come back to him. He nodded to his co-pilot, who did not nod back because he was made of plastic like most of the passengers. Then Jitters pressed the button on his intercom and spoke into the microphone.

"Attention please. This is your captain speaking. Yes, it's Captain Jitters here. I hope you enjoy your flight on Cheapo Cheapo Airlines to . . . uh . . . Bahrain. Yes, that's it. I think.

"Now I don't want to worry you, but the weather forecast's not too good, and I'm a little rusty, only just returned to service from my nervous break — ah — little holiday."

Inside the cabin the passengers were looking nervous. Wendy Wooley leapt up with a brave smile.

"Don't you worry! Captain Jitters has this fantastic sense of humour! Everything's going to be all right. I'm sure it is!"

In the cockpit, Captain Jitters pressed a few buttons and

moved a few levers, and the great plane shuddered and started to move.

"Well," said Captain Jitters, "we're taxiing along the runway now, at least I think it's . . . yes, it's got lights on it, actually my eyesight isn't too good, anyway, let's have a go at getting into the air. I should hold tight if I were you, 'fraid I'm not all that good at takeoffs!"

By now everyone in the plane was strapped in tight, pale and shivering. Quite a few of the passengers were crying, and Mrs Atkins was holding tight to the plastic hand of the dummy sitting next to her.

"Marmalade," said Wendy Wooley. "I just want you to know that if we don't, er . . . I mean if the plane, er . . . I just wanted you to know that I've enjoyed being your social worker. I think you're wonderful, Marmalade. There. I've said it."

"Thanks, cock," said Marmalade. "By the way, what happens if I press this little knob here?"

Wendy Wooley's seat belt flew open and she tumbled head over heels down the aisle to the tail end, just as the great plane lurched groggily into the air.

"I got it up! I got it up!" yelled Jitters. "I don't believe it! We're airborne! Who said I'd never fly again?" He spoke into the microphone again. "Well, now, this is Captain Jitters again, and everything's OK. We're cruising at a height of . . . well, it looks like the altimeter's packed up, but we're cruising, we're off the ground, so who cares. This is Captain Jitters signing off with a little song." And Jitters began to croon through the microphone:

"When you fly through the storm,
Keep your wings up high,
And don't be afraid to jump out,
When the wing falls off give a careless laugh . . ."

Wendy Wooley scrambled to her feet and snapped off the intercom. "Just a bit of interference, everything's all right!" she laughed gaily. "Now Hostess Marmalade will pass down the cabin with refreshments!"

Marmalade appeared with a big tray slung round her neck like an ice cream lady in the cinema.

"Peanuts, chocolate, lemonade, ice cream, get your tutti frutti ice cream!" she warbled, tossing the goodies to right and left. Several passengers got dollops of ice cream in their faces.

"Sorry, Penguins, no fish on the tray!" said Marmalade when she reached the two big nuns.

"We're not penguins dear, we're nuns!" said the bigger of the two, whose moustache reminded Marmalade of Sister Purification's.

"Can't fool me, cock," said Marmalade. "I'll get you a tin of sardines later. Anyway, what are two penguins doing on a trans-continental flight?"

"There are always penguins, I mean nuns, in aeroplane disasters, dear," said the other nun.

"Who said this was going to be a disaster?"

"Things always go wrong on Cheapo Cheapo Airlines, dear. Anyway, when it comes to a crisis you can rely on us. Because penguins, I mean nuns, are tough and hard in an emergency."

"Right, cock," said Marmalade, and moved on down the aisle to where Mr and Mrs Atkins were sitting.

"Marmalade, are you sure this plane is all right?" asked Mrs Atkins. "Bits seem to be falling off the wings!"

"Never fear, mother, it's just aerial dandruff," said Marmalade. "Anyway, what are you doing here?"

"Just off to flog a few paintings to the Sheikhs," said her father. "We *are* going to Saudi Arabia, aren't we?"

"Search me, cock," said Marmalade, and moved on to the

row behind, where a very tense looking businessman with a bushy moustache and dark glasses was clutching a big brief-case on his lap.

"Peanuts, bubblegum, tutti frutti ice cream?" asked Marmalade.

"No thank you. Go away."

"Fancy any other sort of ice cream? Liver and custard?"

"No! Go away!"

"Here, let me put that case on the rack for you, cock."

"*Don't touch the briefcase!*" snapped the businessman, clutching it even more tightly.

"All right, all right, what you got in there, the Crown Jewels?"

"*No!* Now please leave me alone!"

Blinking suspicious character, that, thought Marmalade to herself, as she went back up the aisle.

"Everything all right, Marmalade?" asked Wendy Wooley, who was counting the sick bags.

" 'Course it is. It's a doddle, this job. When do I get the chance to fly this plane?"

Suddenly the intercom crackled and they heard Captain Jitters again.

"Well, ladies, and gentlemen, hope you're enjoying your flight. I've just been in radio contact with London, and let's see, what's the message . . . oh yes, there's a bomb on the plane. All right? Fine. Bye now."

The cabin was in uproar instantly. Passengers were run-ning this way and that, falling over the dummies, looking for the emergency exits, and shouting for their money back.

"Now's our chance to be heroines!" said Wendy Wooley gallantly. "You calm them down, Marmalade, while I see if Captain Jitters has any more information!"

"Back, back, you mutinous dogs!" yelled Marmalade. "The first man up that gangway gets a choc ice in the mush!

Get in your seats, and quick about it!"

The passengers got meekly back into their seats and sat there trembling.

"That's better," said Marmalade. "Only a blinking bomb after all. Blimey, I've been mucking about with bombs since I was in the blinking infants! Now sit still while I come amongst you and do a search!"

Wendy Wooley reached the cockpit just as Captain Jitters was pulling on his parachute.

"Captain Jitters, what can we do?" she cried.

"I don't know what you're going to do, but I'm going to jump!" said the wild-eyed pilot.

"Captain Jitters," said Wendy Wooley with her best Understanding Smile, "please be brave. When we joined this airline, we took on a sacred trust. To take good care of people and carry them safely to lands far away. To give them happy landings, and safe homecomings. Surely you're not going to betray that trust?"

"Oh, all right," said Captain Jitters sulkily. "I'll try. But I'm very very upset about this, and so is Captain Plastic my co-pilot."

Marmalade had searched half the people on the plane already. She hadn't found any bombs, but the more ticklish of the passengers were screaming with laughter. Now she had reached the mysterious businessman with the dark glasses and the moustache.

"Don't touch the briefcase!" he hissed. There was a short dramatic silence and then everyone on the plane heard the sound of ticking coming from the case.

"Aha!" said Marmalade.

The businessman leapt to his feet and tore off his glasses and moustache. Marmalade gasped.

"All right! All right! It was me! Angus Glenfiddick! I am hijacking this plane! I'm going to take my lovely Wendy

83

Wooley to Bonnie Scotland or blow up the lot of you in the attempt!"

He rushed up the aisle towards the cockpit, past the screaming passengers. The two nuns nodded at each other meaningfully, got out their blackjacks, and followed Marmalade up the aisle after him.

"Dr Glenfiddick!" gasped Wendy Wooley, as he burst into the cockpit.

"Yes! Now it is my turn to put myself about! Captain Jitters, I am taking command! Turn about and head for Prestwick, or this little fellow will blow us all to smithereens!"

He produced a small round parcel with a very loud tick and thrust it under Captain Jitters's nose.

"Waaaagh!" said Captain Jitters, and collapsed in a dead faint. Immediately the plane went out of control.

"Quick, Penguins! Hit him with the flippers!" said Marmalade.

And the nuns, who seemed to have lots of practice at this sort of thing, gave Glenfiddick a couple of whacks, and he collapsed unconscious on top of Captain Jitters.

By now the plane was upside down and whirling all over the sky, and the bomb was tumbling about all over the cockpit. After it had rolled up Captain Jitter's trouser leg and out again, Marmalade managed to catch it in her silly hat and throw it out of the window.

"Foiled again! And it was all for you, Wendy!" said Glenfiddick, coming round for a moment.

Wendy Wooley looked down at him tenderly. "Oh, Dr Glenfiddick. You hijacked a whole jumbo jet . . . just for me?"

But it was no good. Glenfiddick was unconscious again. Somewhere down below came the sound of an explosion, and Marmalade peered down.

"Oh, blimey," she said. "We just bombed the Falklands again!"

"Never mind that!" squealed Wendy Wooley. "The plane's out of control! The captain's fainted!"

"Leave it to me," said Marmalade, shoving Jitters out of the way. "Marmalade at the controls at last!"

Wendy Wooley rushed back to the passenger cabin, where the people and the dummies were rolling about all over the plane. "It's all right! Just a spot of turbulence!" she called cheerfully, trying to sort out the arms and the legs. "Soon be back to normal!"

And suddenly, miraculously, it *was* back to normal. The plane levelled out, the passengers scrambled back to their seats, and the intercom crackled.

"Captain Marmalade here, ladies and gentlemen. Situation blinking brilliant. Dead easy, this plane flying. We're coming in to land now, so fasten your seat belts. Doesn't look like Bahrain to me, there's all these great big high buildings. Still, we'll give it a try, cock. Hold on to your hats! Here we go!"

There was a great jolt, followed by the sound of tearing metal. Then the plane stopped. Marmalade turned the engines off and looked out of the window. Funny the plane still seemed to be a long way up. Then Marmalade realised that they were stuck on top of a building. It was a blinking tall building, too. It was the Empire State Building.

"Oh, dear," said Marmalade. And then: "Oh well."

She pressed the button on the intercom.

"Anybody here for New York?"

Shame!

"Weren't you just thrilled to bits with that epic flight?" said Wendy Wooley bouncing into the Atkins livingroom.

"Nearly got *blown* to bits!" said Mr Atkins grumpily.

"Well, she's changed my whole outlook on life," said Wendy Wooley. "Clothes, work, the whole thing. I don't want to be called Miss Wooley any more. I want you to call me . . . Trendy Wendy!"

"No, I don't think I shall do that, Miss Wooley," said Marmalade's mother haughtily. "You must understand that we're very worried about our little girl!"

"Yes, I do understand," said Wendy, hastily putting on her Understanding Smile.

"We're worried she might come back, see," said Mr Atkins.

"Oh, no, Mr and Mrs Atkins, there's no danger of that! I've enrolled her at the New York School of Big-Heads and Show-offs!"

Marmalade mounted the Steps of the New York School for Big-Heads and Show-offs, and stepped through the famous portals. Then she stopped in disgust. The great entrance hall seemed to be chock-full of posers in shiny leotards, singing, dancing, turning cartwheels, crying, discussing their problems, and taking no notice of Marmalade at all.

"Blimey! What a shower!" said Marmalade. "Oy! You lot!

I'm new! Where's the classroom? Where's the toilets?"

They all stopped and turned to stare at Marmalade.

"Who are you, kid?" drawled a handsome big black boy in shiny blue football shorts.

"Marmalade Atkins, cock. I've come to put myself about!"

"Well, baby," he said. "You come to the *right place*!" And all the big-heads and show-offs gathered round Marmalade waving their arms about and waggling their bottoms, and sang her the School Song, which went like this:

"Listen, kid, as you can see,
Coolest cat in school is me!
See me in my dancing suit,
I think I am really cute!
Biggest posers in New York,
Look at me do my fancy walk!
See me laugh and see me cry,
And see me spit in your eye!
Ain't it a SHAME!
We're gonna show off together,
We're gonna dance till we're lame —
SHAME!
Baby you better remember,
Life is a terrible shame!"

Oh, well, thought Marmalade. If it's all going to be singing and dancing here, I'd better blinking well join in. So she jumped on a nearby piano and added a verse of her own:

"Listen cock, I tell you straight,
You have met your blinking fate!
I come here to rave and shout!
I am going to muck about!
You don't know the half I do,

88

Itching powder! Supaglue!
By the end of just one day,
You are going to say — ain't it a
SHAME!
We're at the end of our tether,
Marmalade Atkins the name!
SHAME!
Banging your bonces together,
Ain't that a terrible Shame!
"Shame! Shame! Shame! SHAAAAAAME!"

All the students joined in the final chorus and gathered
around the piano in fancy poses at the climax of the song,
Marmalade felt quite pleased with herself. Mucking about
with this lot was going to be easy. Then a gruff voice rang
out across the hall.

"And vot is the meaning of this?"

All the big-heads and show-offs turned in dismay.

"It's Doctor Shovoffsky!"

"Yes, it's Doctor Shovoffsky," said the old gentleman in
the doorway, peering over his long grey beard. "And you are
late for class!"

"Gee, sorry, Dr Shovoffsky!" said the big-heads and
show-offs. "It was all that new kid's fault, Dr Shovoffsky!
Marmalade Atkins!"

"New kid? Ah, yes, now I see her," said the old gentleman. Welcome to class, little girl. And how can I help
you?"

"Well, I do have one question," said Marmalade. "Is that a
beard, or have you been nicking birds' nests?"

A gasp of horror went up from the students.

"So," said Shovoffsky. "Let us see if you play piano as well
as you play the fool, Miss Atkins."

"As you wish, cock," said Marmalade. She walked over to

the piano and put a small box on top. "Just me little metronome, Dr Shovoffsky. Now how about a bit of Rimsky Caughtacoff?"

"Votever you fish, Miss Atkins."

Marmalade sat down at the piano stool, waggled her wrists, cracked her knuckles, popped her bubble gum, and started to play. A gasp of admiration went up. She was playing the Flight of the Bumble Bee twice as fast as it had ever been played before. Her fingers moved so fast they hardly seemed to touch the keys at all. In ten seconds it was all over. The students cheered, and Dr Shovoffsky jumped up with tears glistening in his beard.

"But zis is Brilliant! And so moving! Kids! We have here with us a genius! Come here, my little samovar, let me shake you by the hand!"

Marmalade strolled proudly over to Dr Shovoffsky. Just as she reached out to take his trembly old hand, the little tape recorder on top of the piano started to play the Flight of the Bumble Bee all over again!

"Er . . . remote control, Dr Shovoffsky!" said Marmalade hopefully, but it was no good. The old music professor burst into tears.

"For this I leave the Moscow Conservatory in 1812? Marmalade Atkins, you have broken my heart!"

And he stumbled out and boo-hooed his way to the canteen, where he needed ten cups of coffee and sixteen apple strudels before he was ready to face the world again.

"Hey, kids!" said a piercing voice. "What goes *down* here?"

It was Starry Isa, the dynamic dance teacher. She perched on the table, swinging her legs, and all the big-heads and show-offs scuttled over and gathered round her feet, gazing up at her adoringly. Marmalade thought she might as well do the same, except that she left out the adoring gaze bit; there was something else she wanted to do.

"You all come to this place because you want *fame*!" yelled Starry Isa, flashing her eyes all over the place like search-lights. "But if you want fame, you gotta *work*! You gotta work till the sweat runs down your nose! Till the tears run down your cheeks! Till your knees buckle and your toes burn!"

"Till your teeth fall out and your nose drops off!" yelled Marmalade, getting into the mood of things.

"Who said that?"

"Me, cock. Marmalade Atkins. Only trying to help."

"And what do *you* know, little limey kid?"

"I know something you don't know," said Marmalade.

"And what is that?"

"You've got itching powder in your leg warmers."

A puzzled look crossed Starry Isa's face. Then her toes began to twitch. Her ankles began to quiver. Her legs began to kick.

"Kids!" said Starry Isa. "When you gotta dance, you gotta dance! Into the fast routine!"

"What do I do, cock?" said Marmalade.

"Baby, you just gotta fit in any way you can!" squealed Starry Isa, who was just beginning to get the full benefit of the itching powder that Marmalade had sprinkled on her leg-warmers. She was twisting, turning, somersaulting and high-kicking, followed in close formation by all the big-heads, show-offs and posers. Marmalade fitted in any way she could, sticking her foot out here and there and giving the occasional little shove. In half a minute, all the big-heads and show-offs were lying in a neat pile in the middle of the dance studio and Marmalade was sitting on top.

"Kids," said Starry Isa. "I don't know whether to laugh, or cry, or shoot myself! — Kids — I think we found a new star!"

When the big-heads and show-offs had recovered from

their dance lesson, they decided it was time to make friends with the new star.

"Hi, Marmalade," said the big black boy with the shiny shorts. "My name's Roy Lee. I used to be the baddest cat in this school till you came along. This chick is Milly and this dude is Billy."

"Hi Marmalade," said Billy and Milly. "Glad to have you on the team. We think you're just great, Marmalade."

"Yuk," said Marmalade.

"My daddy drives a taxi," said Billy. "What does your Daddy do, Marmalade?"

"Well, he's a swindler," said Marmalade. "He's quite good at it. In fact, he's sort of a millionaire."

"Wow! A millionaire!" chorused the big-heads and show-offs.

"Interesting," said a voice behind them. Marmalade turned. Three men were looking at her. They all had striped suits, big hats and evil faces, and the one in the middle had the biggest hat and the meanest face of all.

"Interesting!" he said. "Ain't it, boys?"

"Sure is, Big Julie," they said, and walked off menacingly.

"Who are those geezers?" asked Marmalade.

"Big Julie's gang," said Roy Lee. "Heavy cats."

"The school has to pay them protection money," said Milly.

"Yeah, or they'll burn the school down!" said Billy.

"And now we've run out of money to pay them," said Roy Lee. "Unless somebody do something, this whole school gonna close down!"

"Oh, dear, what a shame," said Marmalade. "Why don't you do a show to raise the money? I mean, that's what you always do, isn't it?"

"Wow! A show!" chorused the big-heads and the show-offs. "What a great idea! And Marmalade can be the star!"

"Sorry kids," said the deep voice behind her. "We got other plans for Marmalade. OK boys — get her!"

Marmalade found herself suddenly lifted off her feet by two men in striped suits, and before the big-heads and show-offs could do anything about it, she had been bundled outside and into the back seat of a huge black car with smoked glass windows, and squashed in between two huge striped suits as the car hurtled through the New York streets.

"Nice car you got here cock," said Marmalade.

"This ain't no car, this is Big Julie's limousine!" said Big Julie. "Enjoy! Because this is maybe the last ride you ever take!"

Both of Big Julie's henchmen laughed in a nasty and meaningful way. They were called Small Sam and Average Al, and they were a couple of very tough cookies.

"Where we going then cock?" asked Marmalade.

"My secret hideout," said Big Julie. "Where no one will ever find you. All my life I been dreaming of a snatch like this. You gonna stay with me till your rich English Daddy pays a million dollar ransom!"

"Suits me," said Marmalade. "I always wanted to get in with the bad guys."

Big Julie's hideout was a fortified boiler-room in the cellars of a Chinese restaurant. Besides a lot of boilers and pipes there was a comfortable sofa, a fridge full of cream cheese, jelly and pop, and an old-fashioned juke box. Marmalade felt quite at home there.

"OK," said Big Julie. "Now we're going to play a little game with some dice. You ever play before?"

"Don't think so," said Marmalade.

"That's fine," said Big Julie. "Small Sam, get this kid's millionaire Daddy on the line, while the kid and Big Julie play crap. Now, listen, kid. You got two dice, and the

93

number you try to get is the seven. And Big Julie shoots first!"

Big Julie took the dice in his big hand that looked like a bunch of bananas, wound himself up, shut his eyes, muttered to himself, and rolled the dice.

"Tough pastrami, boss," said Small Sam and Average Al. "Eight. You nearly got it!"

"Now you, kid," said Big Julie. Marmalade rolled the dice. Everyone waited with baited breath for them to stop rolling. One was a two. The other was a three.

"Seven!" said Marmalade. "I win!"

Big Julie scratched his head. "You sure kid?"

"Sure I'm sure!" said Marmalade. "See, here's a two, you take that two from the six, and that's a four, and here's a three, you take the three from the six you get a three, right?"

"Right," said Big Julie.

"And a four and a three is seven, right?"

"Right!" said Big Julie. "I never figured it that way before!"

"You got any money?" said Marmalade.

"Not right now," said Big Julie.

"That's all right, I'll have your watch," said Marmalade.

By the time Small Sam had got through to England on the telephone, Marmalade had won seven crap games with special arithmetic, and Big Julie was down to his vest and pants. He grabbed the phone with relief.

"OK Mr Atkins," he said. "This is Big Julie in the underwear. I mean the hideout. We got your kid locked up here. You wire a million bucks to Big Julie, or you never see the kid again!"

"Big Julie," said Mr Atkins, "that sounds like a good deal to me."

"Big Julie danced up and down with delight.

"I got myself a deal! I got myself a deal!"

"That's right," said Mr Atkins. "I'll keep the million dollars, and you keep Marmalade. Afternoon, squire."

Big Julie dropped the phone and burst into tears.

"It ain't no good," he said. "All my life I tried to play the big shot, all my life it's gone wrong. I had my problems. I had my hangups. How would you like a name like Julie? I did my best. But I am a failure as a bad guy. What am I gonna do?"

"Well, cock," said Marmalade. "You could try being a good guy."

"A good guy?" said Big Julie. "I never thought of that."

"Come back with me," said Marmalade, "And help me Save the School!"

All was chaos and depression at the New York for Big-heads and Show-offs. Five minutes to opening time for the great fund-raising show, but no star. Starry Isa was weeping in one corner, Dr Shovoffsky was weeping in another, when suddenly there was a great tearing sound and a huge black limousine drove straight through the back scenery.

"Roll up the curtain, folks! Marmalade's back!"

Marmalade and the Bad Guys were the sensation of New York. The Machine Gun Dance brought the audience to its feet, the comedy number — *I may be a dimmo but look at my limo* — had them rolling in the aisles. And there was not a dry eye in the house when Marmalade and Big Julie in their gangster suits linked arms and led the chorus into the big finale, which went like this:

"Even a Bad Guy . . . got Heart!
You might be robbing a bank
When those teardrops start
That ain't a lump of granite

Beating under my coat
And pussycats and bunnies
Bring a lump to my throat!
Even a bad guy . . . got Heart!
Even a big palooka can feel Cupid's dart
So when you're drugged, when you're bugged
When you're even being mugged
Remember Bad guys
And Bad Girls . . .
Bad guys got a great big HEART!

There was deafening applause, the cameras clicked, and the dollars showered on to the stage. Dr Shovoffsky came forward with tears rolling down his cheeks and held up his hands for silence.

"Kids . . . people . . ." he said. "I guess we made it. Your generous donations have saved the school! And who do we have to thank for all this? Marmalade Atkins and Big Julie! Now come along, Marmalade and Julie, don't be shy . . . where are they?"

In the back of Big Julie's limousine Marmalade and Big Julie were dividing up the takings.

"Right, that's three thousand for you, and three thousand for me . . ." said Marmalade.

"Hey," said Big Julie. "Ain't that six thousand you got there?"

"You take the three from the six and what do you get?" said Marmalade.

"You get a three?"

"That's right, Big Julie."

"Oh, yeah," said Big Julie. "I never did count so good."

"That's why you need Marmalade on the job, cock," said Marmalade Atkins.